Blackburn

THE RED HORSE HAUNTING

THE RED HORSE HAUNTING

Ann Wigley

Allen Junior Fiction

Published in Great Britain in 1991 by
J A Allen & Co. Ltd.
1 Lower Grosvenor Place
London SW1W OEL

British Library Cataloguing in Publication Data
Wigley, Ann
Red horse haunting.
I. Title
823.914 [F]

ISBN 0851315453

Prologue

I have always thought of myself as a very ordinary, down-to-earth, well balanced sort of person. My name is Rachel Downing, I am fourteen years old, I have brown hair, brown eyes and I am sensible. Or at least, that's what I am always being told!

"Let Rachel sort it out, she's very sensible, you know," is a phrase that I hear all too often.

Be that as it may, one thing is certain: I am not the dreamy, poetic type, given to imagining things or prone to wild flights of fancy. I could hardly have survived all my childhood years in a racing stables if I were. Racehorses can be highly strung and temperamental, and they are very valuable animals, so it's no use going around with your head in the clouds and your mind on something else when dealing with them.

My Uncle Derry, my father's brother, has a large, successful racehorse training yard in Lambourn. Uncle Derry never married, so he and my parents share the rambling old house behind the stables and I grew up surrounded by tall, thoroughbred racehorses. I thought that it was perfectly normal to be thrown up onto the back of a horse that was far too big for me, and to be told to get on with riding it.

The stable 'lads' soon taught me to be sensible, to take responsibility, to be realistic, to pay attention to detail and to stay calm in a crisis and cope on my own. They may be called 'lads', but most of them are grown men with a long life-time's experience of dealing with valuable racehorses, and they don't suffer fools gladly. I had to do the jobs properly or not at all. I love the beautiful, courageous thoroughbreds and my life would have been only half a life without them, so I became a quick learner.

Uncle Derry says that I have 'the gift' where horses are concerned. The gift of being able, as he puts it, to 'get under a horse's skin', to get the feel of the animal, to tune in to what it is thinking, to ride it with tact and sympathy so that it gives of its best. By the time I was twelve years old I was riding work regularly for my uncle on the gallops, and helping with the schooling and training of the young horses. I shared their in-bred urge to race at speed, to fly over the fences and to win. My burning ambition was to be a jockey.

Horses are great levellers, and it's no use being big-headed about a gift; either you are born with it or you are not, and no credit to you one way or the other. As I have said, I am a very down-to-earth, sensible person, and I accepted, with calm good sense, my father's edict that he would never, ever, allow me to race. My father had been badly hurt in a riding accident when he was a boy, and his father before him had broken his back in a fall when steeplechasing. Dad was reasonable enough to allow me to ride, but racing was definitely forbidden.

Reluctantly, I learnt to ride with my stirrups let down from racing length, and joined the Pony Club. I enjoyed all the activities from mounted games to show jumping, dressage and one day events, and was a member of most of our branch teams at one time or another. Uncle Derry gave me Red Flame for my thirteenth birthday.

Flame is incredibly well bred and a deep, glowing red-chestnut colour, just like his famous father, Red Fire, who won many steeplechases before he was retired to stud. Flame was an undersized first foal who never grew tall enough to race but, at fifteen-one hands high, he was just right for me. Bearing in mind that Flame was bred to steeplechase, and sometimes he gets a little frustrated by being a Pony Club pony, denied his instinct to take off at high speed and get his nose in front of everyone else, he is an uncomplicated little horse and just as sane and sensible as I am.

So, given all this sanity and good sense on both sides, why did all those odd things happen to Flame and myself last summer? Did we both imagine them, or were they real? Quite honestly I've never believed in all the hocus-pocus of ghosts, stepping back in time, echoes from the past and the rest of it. My parents thought that I was just going through a mixed-up, adolescent phase, romanticising ordinary things, confusing day-dreams with reality; maybe they were right.

But, I'll tell you this: if I was suffering from an over-heated imagination, so then was Flame. He sensed it. He felt the fear. He shared my experiences and he played his part on that final, moonlit night. The only thing I can do is to write it all down, right from the beginning, and let you make up your own mind.

ONE

"Well, there it is, Rachel, what do you think of it?" Dad asked. My father is what is known as a 'computer wizard'. He often works away from home for weeks at a time, setting up computer systems, devising computer programs or sorting out computer problems. His latest assignment was at a town deep in the West Country, miles from Lambourn, and would take him a year or more to complete, so he decided to take Mum and me with him.

I told him that the cottage looked very nice and tried not to show how homesick I was feeling. Mum was scrambling out of the car, exclaiming over how beautiful the village was and how she had always wanted to live in a thatched cottage. This one looked a bit ancient and pokey to me, and I was already looking with far more interest at the paddock that lay to one side of and behind Bridge Cottage. It was typical of my thoughtful father to realise that I could never be truly happy anywhere without my horse, and he had gone to a great deal of trouble to find a house to rent that had a couple of acres of land with it.

Mum and Dad vanished inside the cottage, and the lights came on in the crooked little windows to emphasise the softly approaching dusk of the July evening outside. It made me think of Evening Stables in the yard at home, the comfortable, peaceful bustle as the lads settled the horses for the night, the best time of day in the yard, I thought, and a time that I had not missed once in years. I decided to explore the paddock, rather than upset my parents by looking weepy.

Swallowbridge village straggles along the lane from Meadford Cross towards Winterford, and Bridge Cottage stands on the last of the high ground at its northern end, just before the land drops away to the flat waste of Winterford Moor. Swallowbridge must be a very old village, judging by its chocolate box type thatched cottages, the squat Norman church and the ancient manor house standing with faded dignity in what is left of its park, resigned now to a new role in life as a nursing home.

With the house agent's details in my hand, I paced the boundary of Flame's new home and my spirits rose slightly. The view of open fields all round was beautiful, with Trickett's Hill, as it was called on my map, rising to the south, and the vista of moor stretching away to the north. Bridge Cottage faced east, onto the lane, and the two acre paddock was L-shaped, bordering the road on the right hand side of the cottage, then angling behind the house and up a slight rise, to where glimpses of a wall and a roof showed through a massive clump of trees and creepers. The western and northern boundaries of the two acre field were skirted by a brook that gurgled and chuckled under the bridge, further down the lane, and which gave Bridge Cottage its name.

Flame would not be joining us in Swallowbridge until we had settled in and organised a stable for him, because he is not used to living out all the time. I had left him in his box in Uncle Derry's yard only that morning, all tearful goodbyes on my part, but he just got on with eating his hay and was quite unmoved. People write a lot of romanticised nonsense about horses loving their owners so much that they are devastated by parting. Devastated Flame most definitely was not! We like and respect each other, or rather, I love him while he likes and respects me, and we have a lot of fun together. But Flame is a very prosaic horse who knows on which side his manger is filled, so to speak, and has a healthy appreciation of the hand that holds the bucket. Flame is constitutionally strong and a good doer to the point of being greedy, so Uncle Derry would be his hero until he had to depend on me again.

I wandered along the roadside boundary of the paddock until I met the brook, then followed it to the point where it curved along the western edge of the field. It was a pretty little stream, quite wide but fairly shallow, no more than knee deep, even in the middle, flowing gently but purposefully between its reedy banks to drain into Winterford Moor. On the far side was a stout hedge that had the crew-cut, chunkily wide look of being chopped by a machine, rather than cut and thinned by hand. It reminded me of the schooling fences on Uncle Derry's gallops at home.

As I stood at the water's edge, with the shadow of the hedge lengthening towards me from the after-glow of the setting sun, I began to shiver and was overcome by the weirdest feeling. It was the half-excited but more than a little scared feeling of riding into a dauntingly big jump, and not being at all sure that my horse would clear it. Jumping had never frightened me before; I could not understand it.

Then I was sweating the cold sweat of terror, with panic prickling the hairs on the back of my neck. I felt compelled to look down into the grey water, and found myself choking on a scream. It was pulling me down. I was breathless, crushed by a great weight, and my lungs were bursting with the pain of not being able to draw my breath. I was almost on the point of passing out, when my good sense took control and I began to fight.

Step by faltering step I struggled to back away from the water's edge, needing all my strength to break the hold of whatever strange force was compelling me into the water. Then, suddenly, I was free. I spun round and ran for my life, not heeding where I was going.

A high wall brought me up short and I leaned against it shaking, my ribs heaving to drag in great swallows of air. The panic terror gradually subsided, but left me weak and confused. I was amazed at myself. I could not think what had come over me. Then I began to laugh, a little shakily, at my own foolishness. I looked around me. It was a calm, beautiful evening, holding nothing of fear or threat, and the horizon was rosy-pink and peaceful behind the harmless little stream.

I took comfort from the rough, sun-warmed texture of the reassuringly normal red brick wall. Then I forgot my fright in the excitement of realising what was hidden behind the wall.

'Former stables and stores in need of repair', it said in the agent's brochure. That must be the roof I had seen through the trees on the side of the paddock, behind Bridge Cottage. I began to poke my way along the overgrowth of brambles and trailing ivy, to find a way in.

The double wooden doors were massively high and wide, and stoutly studded with ornate metal bosses. It took me a while to locate them because they faced north, looking across the paddock, rather than towards Bridge Cottage, as if trying to disassociate their grandeur from the humble little dwelling. Grand they might have been once, but now the doors were crumbling with rot, their hinges weak from rust and age. One had given way altogether so that one of the doors leaned inwards; its weight had snapped the ancient, padlocked chain that had sealed them shut for who knows how long. The gap between the doors was just wide enough for me to wriggle through.

Beyond was a little stable yard, and it was perfect. To either side, high walls enclosed the cobbles and, at the back, was a long, gable-ended building: two stables and a store room below, with a hay loft above. Unfortunately, the 'in need of repair' was a typical estate agent's understatement. The place was derelict.

The stable doors were just splintered remains dangling from ornate but rusted hinges. In the centre of the yard stood a moss-encrusted stone trough with a coat of arms carved on its side and a pump at one end. There were gaping holes in the creeper-strangled roof, and the cobbles had all but vanished under a mass of docks, nettles and tangled grass. But I loved it. I imagined it mended, painted and restored to its former grandeur, with Flame's head looking out over one of the half doors. I felt the first stirring of pleasure and excitement.

"Well, what do you think of it?" Dad had come silently up the weed-covered path from the cottage, and made me jump. "Soon get it all fixed up, then Flame can join us here. I've asked a local builder to start work on it as soon as possible."

I was ripping handfuls of grass from the handle of the old pump and cranking it up and down. It wheezed and clanked, but coughed up nothing more than dust and dead leaves. Dad laughed.

"Come on, Rachel. We'd best be getting back to the hotel. Heavy day tomorrow when the furniture arrives!"

We walked arm in arm, down the path from the stables to the cottage, and I was feeling far less miserably homesick for Lambourn and Uncle Derry's yard. There was the whole of the summer holidays to look forward to, in this pretty village. There were bound to be other horsy people I could make friends with, bridleways for Flame and me to explore and horse shows to go to. I would be independent in my stately home of a stable yard, and I could make my own plans.

I had for the moment forgotten my inexplicable, terrifying experience by the brook. The pulse-hammering, breath-stopping terror had gone completely out of my mind. If I am really psychic, as Cathy Trent later kept telling me I was, surely I would have felt some ghastly premonition then, but I did not. I went away, laughing and chatting with Dad, obliviously happy, while it waited for me, brooding and silent with menace by the grey water.

TWO

By eleven o'clock the next morning, I'd had as much as I could take of moving in. I claimed for my own the little back bedroom with the sloping ceiling and the dormer window. It was the smallest of the three bedrooms, but it looked across the paddock to the stables where Flame would live, and gave me a breathtaking view over the brook and the green fields to Tricketts Wood. It did not take me long to unpack.

Mum, on the other hand, was having the time of her life arranging things and being indecisive. Bridge Cottage was let furnished, but the 'few odds and ends' that Mum could not exist without nearly filled a removals van, and the bemused sweating removals men were lugging her pride-and-joy-chaise-longue into its umpteenth different position when I escaped.

The first thing I wanted to do was to explore properly the derelict stable yard. I ran up the slight incline to the weedy path behind Bridge Cottage, and gave the leaning door a hefty shove. I should have been more patient and wriggled through the gap as before. I do not know for how long the single rusted hinge had been holding it, years probably, but my shove was obviously the last straw. The tall, heavy door crashed down inside the yard, reverberating, bouncing and splintering before it settled, bringing a shower of leaves and ivy with it.

Even as the echo died in the enclosed space, I heard above it a frantic, high-pitched whinny and the rattle of hooves scrabbling on stones. It came again, the shriek of a frightened horse and the sound of a struggle, from somewhere behind the stable building. There was no other way round, so I had to get across the yard.

By the time I had pushed my way through the nettles and brambles, I was stung and scratched all over and not feeling particularly sympathetic, even though the animal sounded as if it was in trouble. Behind the stables, a three-sided brick enclosure, the site of the long-rotted muck heap, filled the gap between the building and a hedge, and through the hedge I could just make out the shape of a horse throwing itself about in panic. A few more scratches later and I was through the hedge grabbing for its bit.

He was jet black, rather handsome and immensely tall, probably, I thought, over seventeen hands high. He was saddled and bridled, with his stirrups swinging as he plunged. His trailing reins were caught in the hedge and held him a frightened prisoner. I smoothed his neck as I spoke to him gently, and released his head. His ears flicked nervously, he was streaming with sweat and his flanks were trembling. I guessed that it had been the noise I made demolishing the door that had scared him so much, but he must have lost his rider and been running loose for some time before that, otherwise his jockey would have been lying about somewhere, and there was no one in sight.

We were standing on the bridleway which ran from the Swallowbridge lane, past the back of my stable yard to the open fields, then Trickett's Drove beyond. I set off towards the village, with the black horse jibbing and spooking beside me and getting, if anything, into a far worse state of terror. It was as much as I could do to hold onto him.

The bridleway met the lane beside the village pub, the Lark Rising Inn, and I hammered on the door, while the black jerked at his reins and churned circles in the car park.

"Ain't a clue," the man who answered the door and my question said. "Never seen it before, must be new in the village. You'd best ask at Liz Trent's place, the Rectory Stables—a no through road on the right, called Blind Lane, a mile down the lane towards Meadford Cross."

A mile-long walk leading the black was not funny. I soon had bruised ribs and crushed toes to add to the discomfort of my scratches and stings. The stupid horse was getting on my nerves. I couldn't imagine what had happened to get him into such a lather, and I began to worry about his rider.

At last I found Blind Lane, and a little way down it on the right, a red-brick archway led into a cobbled yard. The black plunged and clattered through the gate which bore a sign, 'The Rectory Livery Stables'.

"Good grief, it's King Kong," a girl about my own age, with a blonde bob of hair, looked up, startled, from forking the muck heap by the wall. "Where on earth did you find him in that state?"

"On the bridleway behind the pub," I said, "there was no sign of his rider, and something had scared him out of his wits. I think there must have been an awful accident."

A slight, red-headed girl came out of one of the stables. "That means Amanda is either gasping her last on Trickett's Drove or legging it home by now. Either way, she's not going to be very pleased," she said. She didn't sound very concerned.

"Owzat?" howled a voice behind me, and a blurr of black jeans, flopping hair and outlandishly printed T-shirt hurtled under the gate arch and launched a cricket ball with vicious ferocity into the yard. A very tall boy, standing in the middle of the cobbles, swiped with a shovel and thumped the ball into the wall behind me. The black horse screamed and stood straight up on his hind legs.

The two girls dived for the horse's head, but even our combined strengths were not enough, and we were towed unceremoniously a couple of times round the yard before we dragged him to a halt.

"The thoughtless freak in black is my older brother Charlie," the blonde girl said, "he doesn't really understand horses. I'm Cathy Trent, we live here."

"Or to be more precise, Charlie hates horses!" the red-headed girl added sourly, "And he can be a flaming nuisance. I'm Virginia Barker, call me Vinny, and the bean-pole over there is Rich—Richard Mason. He's a lot less stupid than Charlie because he's been semi-civilised by horses."

"I don't think any philosopher has ever defined 'civilised' as spending hours a day mucking out dungy stables," Charlie protested. He grinned a vacuous grin at me through his bleached fringe. "Sorry I spooked the animal. Don't suppose you're that priceless rarity, a girl who doesn't ride and likes cricket?" he asked.

I had to admit that, sorry, I wasn't. My name was Rachel Downing and I'd spend all day in the saddle given half a chance. My words came in gasps as the black horse chucked his head from side to side, and tried to dig holes in the cobbles with his crashing front feet.

"He's usually quite sane, dozy even," Vinny panted, doing her share of hanging on. "I can't think what's got into him!"

Between us, we managed to manoeuvre the huge King Kong into his box and I discovered, from the name plate on its door, that he was really called Ebony King, but I could see the reason for his nick-name. We tried to rub him down and settle him, but he just sweated up all over again. In the end, we found him a sweat-rug that fitted only where it touched, and left him to ponder whatever demented thoughts were bothering him.

"Right, hadn't we better get a move on and look for Amanda?" I asked. There was silence.

"Ah," Rich said eventually.

"Well," said Vinny.

"S'pose so," Cathy said.

"I'm off back to the house then," Charlie declared.

"He doesn't ride much," Cathy explained, rather unnecessarily.

"I don't ride AT ALL," Charlie shouted, "I've got

more sense!" and he slouched away under the gate arch. It struck me that Cathy's older brother had very little sense, as I watched him mooch away up Blind Lane to the Rectory, a scare-crow figure bowling imaginary cricket balls at the fence posts. I didn't think I was going to like Charlie Trent very much.

"You see," Rich said to me, "Amanda is not the sort of person to smother you with gratitude for rescuing her. Quite the opposite, especially if she knows we know she's fallen off!"

"Serves her right if she has," Vinny said, callously. "She needs teaching that she's not God's gift to the horse world after all. She's always had to go one better than everyone else in the Pony Club, always ponies that were too big for her, flashy performance jobs too. She's had King Kong only a week, and I'm sure she bought him just because he's built like a tower block and she can look down on everyone."

"Well," I said, "she must be a very good rider if she can cope with him."

"She is," Cathy sighed. "That's the trouble, she's brilliant but she never lets us forget it. To be perfectly honest, we're all being beastly jealous and hoping she's come a cropper at last. We should be ashamed of ourselves."

"I'm not!" Vinny scowled.

"We couldn't do without her in the Pony Club teams," Rich admitted, "but doesn't she know it!"

"She couldn't do without us either," Vinny said, indignantly. "Even Amanda can't be a team on her own, can she?"

I understood how they felt and I sympathised. Every

Pony Club branch has at least one Amanda, who is good at everything and has fantastic ponies, but who is big-headed and incapable of mucking in, so not at all likeable. It is a fact that one just has to live with, but no excuse for leaving them crushed and broken on a remote bridleway, and I said as much.

Rich declared that I must be a far nicer person than he was, a candidate for sainthood in fact. Vinny pointed out that it was easy for me to talk because I'd never actually met Amanda, had I? And Cathy suggested that I borrow a hat and a horse and join the search, because it was my idea anyway. She saddled Fred for me, a stocky, brown fourteen-three hand pony that she was looking after for a friend, and we set off.

We started our search where I had found King Kong, on the bridleway behind my stables, then followed the bridleway until it joined Trickett's Drove, and rode for an hour in each direction. We never found a squashed Amanda because she was already at home, quite unhurt and happy in the knowledge that her horse had been returned safely. Cathy's mother, Liz Trent, who owned and ran the Rectory Stables, had rung her to tell her so. It was just as well, because we were too busy talking and getting to know each other to conduct a very thorough search.

Vinny's effervescent personality seemed almost too big for her tiny frame, which was slight and as small-boned as a bird. She kept up a constant stream of exuberant chatter, wanting to know all about me in the friendliest way, but I had the impression that she believed in saying bluntly exactly what she thought about anything, and could flare into a temper as fierce as her mass of flaming red hair if provoked.

Vinny's milk-white mare, Pearly, was barely fourteen hands and as finely built as her owner, but fizzed with almost uncontrollable energy. She bounded along, refusing to walk when the other ponies walked, leaping around when we trotted, and becoming just a white whisk of a tail in the distance when we cantered. Vinny sat the plunges with unconcerned ease, and said she liked a pony with a bit of go in it. It seemed to me that Pearly was one of those slightly lunatic, speed merchant ponies, that can so easily become equine delinquents fastened down by a harsh bit and masses of leather, but Vinny rode Pearly in a simple snaffle bit, and controlled her with amazing tact and skill. Vinny and Pearly were, Rich told me, the Pony Club speed jumping stars, and I could well believe it.

Rich and Vinny were next door neighbours who lived in Winterford, liveried their ponies at the Rectory and had known each other all their lives. Rich was tall and lanky, with a shock of brown hair, kind eyes and freckles. He was, at fifteen, a year older than Vinny and seemed uncommunicative only when Vinny was in full flow. He had obviously long since given up trying to get a word in edgeways at such times. However, he would take only so much of Vinny's bossing, and they had frequent arguments which they both appeared thoroughly to enjoy.

The greatest sadness in his life, Rich told me, was that he had so quickly outgrown his fourteen-two pony, The Wizard. The Wizard was a mysterious, smokey, blue-roan colour, with quality, substance and a wise expression. He had been handed down from one to the other by the Mason children, but Rich was the youngest. When Rich found a new horse, and his mother threatened a sixteen hand cobby type at the very least, the much loved family pony would have to be sold. The prospect was making Rich wretchedly miserable.

Cathy Trent seemed the quietest of the three, but I put this down to the fact that her fifteen-hand, liver chestnut gelding, Talisman, was only six years old, still a little green and inclined to behave unpredictably. She could not afford to let her attention wander when her mount might, at any minute, shy at a rustle in the hedge and leap sideways. But, she said, his flatwork was improving all the time and his love of jumping excused him any immature nerves from which he still suffered.

Despite her close attention to Talisman, Cathy must have been listening while Vinny extracted from me my entire life history, and a detailed description of Flame and all we had done in our Pony Club teams at home. When it came to the point of explaining why Flame had stayed behind with Uncle Derry, Cathy cut into the conversation.

"But that's stupid. You can't wait half the summer holidays without your horse, while a builder takes his time. We've got a few spare boxes in the yard, and I know Mum would be only too pleased to lend one to a neighbour."

"You could stable Flame at the Rectory," Rich agreed, "and turn him out in your paddock at Bridge Cottage."

"And," Vinny spun round excitedly in her saddle, making Pearly side-step and buck, "you could be in the Rectory Stables' team for the Chawton Show. It's the perfect excuse to get rid of Amanda. I mean, we don't even know yet if her monster horse can jump."

"He won't have to," Rich grinned. "He'll just step over the fences, and don't be so catty, Vin, Amanda's always been in the team, and we won it last year."

"Well, according to her, SHE won it," Vinny snapped. "We just tagged along for the ride and humble privilege of watching an expert jump."

"It wouldn't be fair anyway," I protested, "for me to muscle her out of the team, when I've only just arrived and you've known her for years. What team?"

"We've only known her for years because we haven't had any choice," Vinny sulked. "She's a big-headed. . . ."

"Oh, do shut up, Vin," Rich ordered, and Vinny made a face at him.

Rich then explained to me that the big county-standard Chawton Show always held a four-horse, team jumping competition, split into junior and senior sections, that had become something of a needle match between the local equestrian centres, riding clubs and various riding schools and livery yards in the area. Last year, the Rectory Team of Cathy, Rich, Vinny and Amanda had won the junior section, and they were desperately keen to do so again before Rich was too old for the class. They had, Vinny said, grown rather attached to the challenge cup as well, which was a pretty impressive monster.

By the time we returned to the Rectory, my whole summer had been planned for me. It was taken for granted that Flame would arrive just as soon as Uncle Derry could start up his horsebox, and that I would transfer, without delay, to the Meadford Vale branch of the Pony Club. There would be masses of room, Vinny said, expansively, for Flame in the lorry that Liz Trent hired if lots of people in the yard wanted to go to the same show, and there were plenty of shows coming up. I had my doubts about the team jumping competition, but kept quiet in the face of Vinny's unstoppable enthusiasm.

THREE

I lingered late that evening in the tack room at the Rectory Stables, because it was such a pleasant, sociable place to be at the end of an enjoyable day. Saddle racks, lockers and kit trunks lined the walls; battered, jumble-sale armchairs were grouped round the unlit stove at one end of the room, and the air was full of the rich, warm smell of well soaped leather and the aroma of coffee. I forgot that I was tired and hadn't eaten since breakfast, while Cathy introduced me to the other liveries who had gathered to gossip after evening stables. My homesickness for Lambourn was fading fast.

As Cathy had predicted, Mrs Trent was more than happy to lend a stable for Flame, and she insisted that I contact Uncle Derry as soon as possible, but she was surprised to learn that there were stables at Bridge Cottage. Neither the Trents nor anyone else in the room knew of the existence of my little yard. It was hardly surprising though, if it had been lost for who knows how long behind the chained and overgrown doors.

"Fancy just leaving them to fall to bits like that!"

Rich exclaimed. "What a waste, when there are always masses of people crying out for somewhere to keep a horse."

"I bet they're creepy and spooky," Vinny said, "all ruined and deserted, especially in the dark! I'd love to see them before the builder spoils the scary effect."

"They're not spooky," I laughed. "just weedy!"

"Well I want to see them anyway," Vinny insisted.

I felt a small twinge of annoyance, when Vinny jumped to her feet and chivied the others into walking home with me to see the stables. I had been looking forward to exploring them on my own. I wanted to savour the investigating and planning by myself, and for my foot to be the first over the threshold after so long a gap in time, as it would have been that morning if the tall black horse hadn't intervened, but there is no stopping Vinny when she has one of her enthusiasms. I told myself that I shouldn't be so selfish, after these new friends had welcomed me to the village in such an easy, generous way. Of course, the shared experience of being trampled all over by King Kong had helped to break the ice between us.

A noisy group of small children was playing in the lane in front of Bridge Cottage and Mum was leaning on the garden gate, talking to their mothers. She looked weary and dishevelled, but triumphant, and I wondered if her chaise-longue was still on the move or finally settled, probably in the first position that she had tried. She told me that supper would be very late, so we would have plenty of time to explore the stables.

"Wow, talk about delusions of grandeur, whoever built this meant it to be pretty impressive," Rich said, gazing up at the two massive stone pillars that held the yard doors. He grabbed an armful of trailing creeper, and hauled down a blanket of ivy from the top of one of them. The remaining yard door began to sway precariously.

"Just look at that dressed stonework, and there's some kind of carving on it too. This was definitely a 'money no object' project," Vinny said.

"Not a bit what you'd expect to find behind a humble, thatched cottage," Cathy agreed. "There has to be a story to it, don't you think?"

We tramped through the gap in the wall, and the fallen wooden door cracked and broke up under our tread. Cathy and Rich found sticks to whack their way through the nettles, but Vinny forged ahead regardless.

"These two loose boxes are enormous," she called, "far bigger than normal. I wonder why?"

"You know, it's not half as bad as it looks," Rich said, peering up at the roof of the gable-ended building. "I don't think it's so very old after all. All the beams are sound. It just needs new battens and tiles, and all new doors, of course." He kicked at a swinging stable door and it disintegrated.

"Vandal," Vinny said. "Can I do the same with this one? It must be the tack room, but its padlocked."

"Go ahead," I said. "The builder will have to bash it down anyway."

Vinny lunged her shoulder at the door, which was so rotten that even her slight weight was enough to wrench it off its hinges. It slumped drunkenly inwards, and a wave of cold, stale air flowed out of the dark room.

"Pooh," Rich said, "It smells like nobody's been in here for centuries!"

"Thought you said it wasn't that old after all," Vinny

contradicted him, and we all followed her inside.

The window in the back wall was grimed and festooned with cobwebs, so that only a little of the evening light managed to filter into the room. It took our eyes a while to adjust to the gloom, and then we saw the chaos. The place looked as if it had been turned upside down.

Rusted feed bins lay toppled under the window, their sides savagely dented by the force of their falling. A shelf and a cupboard slanted down from one wall, obviously ripped violently from their places, rather than decaying with time. Their contents were tumbled across the floor, to mingle with the fragments of an age-blackened oil lamp and its shattered glass funnel. The charred remains of a horse blanket covered a scorch mark on the floor round the lamp. My mouth was dry and I began to shiver.

"I'd say someone had the most amazing fight in here!" Rich exclaimed. "This saddle rack has been torn off the wall, screws and all, and hurled across the room by the looks of it."

"They were lucky the whole place didn't go up in flames, too," Cathy kicked at the burnt cloth.

"Nice old hunting whip, but a bit of a monster. Look, the tarnished bit round the top is silver, I think, and its got a crest on it." Vinny picked up the whip from the floor, and its thong and lash disintegrated into dust.

"What about this then?" Rich was testing the weight of a cudgel, tossing it from hand to hand and polishing the wood against his sleeve. The huge, knobbed end winked threateningly in the dim light, and I began to feel sick.

From the minute that I had first stepped through the door, the conviction had been growing in me that this room had an evil atmosphere. I became colder and colder with the feeling that fear was soaking into my skin and hatred was washing round me. It seemed to me that the whole place reeked of vicious violence and cruelty and, by now, I was sure that the rush of foetid air, released when Vinny opened the door, had been witness to some awful scene in the past. I rushed outside and bent over the stone trough, retching helplessly.

"You O.K., Rachel?" Cathy's concerned voice came from behind me. "You've gone as white as a sheet!"

"Sorry," I gasped. "I'll be O.K. in a second. It's just something about that room. I hate it."

"Don't let all the filthy mess upset you," Rich said, kindly. "It can be cleared up soon enough. What say we all give you a hand clearing the weeds tomorrow? Your builder could start cleaning up the building straight away if we did. I'll bring some hooks and rakes over first thing in the morning, if you like."

Everyone thought that this was a good idea and volunteered to help. I didn't like to say that my one overwhelming desire was to chain the place shut as soon as possible, and never return to it again. Then Vinny began to fuss about how late it was getting, and that she and Rich would miss the last bus home to Winterford, if they didn't hurry. I was glad to leave, and led them quickly through the nettles to the gate. As I picked my way over the broken door, a nightmare face loomed out of the shadows in front of me and I almost stopped breathing.

It was a very old face, its skin deeply wrinkled and blotched with the liver-brown mottling of age. The bald skull was fringed with straggling white hair and, above the sunken, toothless mouth, the eyes were wide with terror but blazing with accusing fury. I stopped dead and Cathy cannoned into my back, stifling a gasp, as startled as I was.

The old man pointed a trembling claw finger at me.

"'Twas you what done it," he quavered "I see'd you do it. You it was what opened the door. It were safely locked and you felled it."

Cathy let out a long breath. "It's only Ben," she said. "Batty Ben from the village, daft as a brush and over ninety, or so he claims!" Her laughter relieved my tension a little. "What are you doing here, Ben?" she asked slowly and clearly.

"Get on home, Ben," Rich said, less sympathetically, "You're trespassing and you frightened the girls."

"He didn't frighten me!" Vinny was indignant.

The old man began to mutter. "The burning is out. The burning is out now." His toothless gums worked against each other in agitation, until spittle ran down his chin and his voice rose to a wail. "The burning is out, the burning is out an' 'twill all happen again, then they'll beat I because of it."

"Don't be stupid," Vinny said "No one's going to beat you for letting a fire go out."

Batty Ben ignored her. He dropped to his knees and began to scrabble at the fallen door, pulling at its edges with manic fingers, but still staring up at me, his eyes desperate.

"It'll take you too, if you don't lock the doors. Lock the doors against the burning or they'll beat I again till my head goes dark." Tears furrowed down Ben's frantic face, and his expression held an abject terror.

He renewed his futile struggle with the door until the blood ran from his broken finger nails.

"You'll never shift that." Rich took hold of Ben's shoulders and tried to pull him to his feet, but the old man fought him off with surprising strength.

"Don't you see?" he sobbed. "The burning. The burning is out!"

"He lost his marbles years ago," Vinny said. "He's just a mixed up old lunatic with a fire fixation. Bet he was a pyromaniac in his youth, that's why someone beat him up!"

"Or he's been at the scrumpy again," Rich agreed. "He swills pints of it at the Lark Rising, and Dad says it rots the brain."

"Go on home then, Ben, and light another fire if it will make you feel better," said Vinny. "Make him get a move on, Rich, or we'll have to go. That bus isn't going to wait for us."

"We can't leave Rachel to cope on her own with the old man, when she's feeling rough anyway," Rich said.

I was not being much help. I was rooted to the spot by cold, trembling dread, and the old man's eyes seemed to bore right through me. It was the look on his face that petrified me, rather than his idiot words. Fool or no fool, it was genuine fear, not old age, that shook Ben's body, while he wrestled with the impossible and tried to lift the door.

"He's not going to do anything if you bully him," Cathy reasoned. "Come on, Ben, it's time to go home, you know." She began to talk gently to the old man, as if he was a small child, and, eventually, she coaxed him to his feet.

Cathy and Rich took an arm each, and began to lead

Batty Ben away down the path. Then, he stopped dead and turned to look at me again.

"You opened the door," he whimpered. "Don't 'ee know about the burning? Was it Georgie what made you do it, like he made I?"

"For heaven's sake, stop talking nonsense, we're in a hurry." Vinny gave Ben a push from behind, to get him moving.

"Take no notice of him, Rachel," Rich called cheerfully over his shoulder. "He never makes any sense. See you tomorrow."

I managed to croak 'goodnight', and watched them out of sight, round the corner of Bridge Cottage. Rich's and Vinny's laughter floated back to me on the warm night air; Cathy's head was bent to talk to the bowed figure of Batty Ben that shambled beside her. I fled indoors.

I couldn't get Batty Ben out of my mind. I found it hard to dismiss him, as the others had done, as just a silly old man wandering in his wits. I bolted my supper, told my parents I was dog tired and took refuge in my room. As I drew my curtains, I glanced across the meadow and he was there.

Batty Ben was back again. The stooped silhouette, its arms hanging slack at its sides and its mouth agape, merged with the shadows near the entrance to the stable yard. It was motionless, and staring fixedly at the doorless gap in the wall.

I had never before found myself in a situation that I couldn't cope with, and I was horrified that the evening's events could reduce me to such a nervous state. I sat on my bed, determined to be sensible about it and pull myself together. I must consider everything logically and reasonably.

The tack room had been abandoned for years, so no wonder it was a mess. Things rot after a long time, they decay and fall down; that was all that had happened. Vinny had gone to the yard expecting it to be a spooky and scary, and she had influenced my subconscious mind. I was being over-imaginative and silly. Of course there was nothing wrong with the tack room that a good cleaning out wouldn't cure.

I had felt sick because I'd been tired and hungry and, for the same reason, I had over-reacted to the sudden appearance of Batty Ben. Obviously the old man was senile and not quite right in the head. There was no meaning at all behind his senseless ramblings. I must put him right out of my mind and stop behaving like a fanciful child.

I had a long, comforting soak in the bath, read two chapters of a very good book and sneaked downstairs to raid the fridge for a second supper. By the time I put out my light, I was relaxed and cheerful again, all terrors forgotten and not worrying any more about the senseless old man, keeping his lonely vigil by the yard gates. I would get Dad to chase Ben away, if he was still there in the morning, and it would be fun, clearing the yard with the others tomorrow.

FOUR

"I'm so glad you've made some friends so quickly," Mum said. She put down the tray of cold drinks and sandwiches on the stone trough, and gazed round my transformed stable yard. Cathy, Vinny and Rich were sitting exhausted and dusty on the cobbles, backs to the stable wall and faces raised to the warm sun, while their ponies, plus Fred, grazed in my paddock. Even Cathy's brother had turned up for a while, looking like a refugee from a jumble sale, and had hooked at the odd weed. His help soon degenerated into silly jokes and Tarzan impressions on the roof, then he got under everyone's feet and fooled about so much that Vinny lost her temper and chased him away with a bill-hook.

We had worked like slaves all morning, and now a huge pile of nettles, grass and ivy wilted by the gate.

"Come on, everybody, have some lunch or you'll be too weak for the Pony Club do this afternoon," Mum laughed, and we scrambled for a much needed drink.

"Not bad, is it, Mrs Downing?" Rich asked, with satisfaction. He had spent hours on the roof, avoiding

Charlie and cutting down the rampant ivy and brambles, while the rest of us cleared the cobbles. I thought he was being far too modest.

"It's amazing. Wonderful. Great," I said, "and I can never thank you enough."

"The builder is bringing a rubbish skip for this lot, this afternoon," Mum informed us. "You've saved him a day's work, and he can start on the buildings right away. Well done everybody."

Knowing that I was transferring to the Meadford Vale Pony Club, the branch secretary, the steely eyed, clarion-voiced Mrs Monica Smith, said I was welcome to attend the rally being held at the Rectory that afternoon. Cathy was lending me Fred again, and warned me that he might be a bit of a handful when it came to jumping, which he loved. It was to be a showjumping instruction rally.

"That's Amanda, over there!" Cathy hissed to me, as we rode into the Rectory car park, which was already overflowing with trailers and riders.

"Can't really miss her, can you?" Vinny giggled. "She's going to need oxygen at that altitude!"

I hardly recognised King Kong as the same, terror-crazed creature that I had wrestled with all the way back from the Lark Rising Inn to the Rectory. He towered above every other horse in the car park, but looked half asleep, with his head hanging and his long ears flopping sideways. The infamous Amanda was cool and sophisticated, a slim, attractive girl in an immaculately tailored jacket and glossy leather boots. She sat easily in her saddle, her seat perfect and her hands light and sensitive on the reins. The impressive picture was spoilt somewhat by her snooty expression. But, then, it's easy to give the impression that you're looking down your nose at everybody, when mounted on something that is on eyeball to eyeball terms with the Empire State Building.

I was in the intermediate ride with Cathy, Vinny, Rich, Amanda and two other people because I, like them, had just passed C + test and was beginning work for B test.

"Oh, I see you've got sweet little Fred," Amanda said, condescendingly to me, as we circled the paddock, waiting for the instructress. Fred's sturdy neck was overbent with excitement, and he'd begun to plunge and fly-buck as soon as he saw the waiting jumps. The energy under my saddle felt neither little nor sweet to me.

"Don't you have your own pony then?" Amanda gave me a superior smirk, and I craned my neck upwards to look at her, as King Kong, with his mile-eating stride, stalked past. I told her I owned a fifteen-one failed race-horse, who would be arriving any day.

"How sweet," the voice came again from on high, and I marvelled at her singular lack of vocabulary.

Within the first ten minutes of the rally, I realised that Mrs Shortland was an exceptionally good instructress: she knew what she was talking about and had the gift of being able to teach, and she brought variety and fun to the familiar routine of warming up and trotting poles. The inevitable grid-work without stirrups produced the usual howls of agony from everyone, but I had half an eye on Amanda, who suffered the additional problem of stopping King Kong, in his seven-league boots, from bumping into all the smaller ponies.

A beaky-nosed, elderly woman was leaning on the paddock railings. She looked every inch the hard-bitten rider to hounds, and was wearing a quilted waist-coat, men's cavalry twill trousers and jodhpur boots, with a flat, waxed cap tilted stylishly over her forehead. She was calling a constant stream of advice to Amanda, then yelling at everyone in turn. "Give her room, you on the grey. Get out of her way, you tall boy, you're crowding. Oh let her pass for heaven's sake, that girl on the common brown pony!"

"It's her Granny," Cathy said to me, while we ducked Talisman and Fred into a corner to let Amanda lope past. "Bane of every working rally, Granny is. She used to hunt a lot, a million years ago, before they invented the forward seat! Thinks she knows it all. Sometimes she gives the instructor a shove and takes over herself."

"Oh lovely, Amanda, BRAVO," Granny trilled, and I could see Mrs Shortland's expression darken.

There was no question about it, Amanda rode exceptionally well. It was such a pity, I thought to myself, that she was so over-horsed. Her heels reached only a little way down King Kong's sides, and he gangled along, poking his nose, trailing his hocks and wearing a puzzled expression. I could sense his confusion, as he tried to work out how the nudges, just below his saddle flaps, were related to the aids, given usually so much lower down his belly. King Kong's brain was, obviously, a lot more modest in size than his body.

We finished the lesson by tackling a line of fences set at related distances, requiring different numbers of strides between each jump. Amanda was really in trouble now. King Kong's stride was half as long again as that of any other pony in the ride, and he crashed, scrambled and smashed his way through the jumps, getting his legs in a tangle and hurting his shins, until his eyes were white-ringed with panic.

Granny dashed into the paddock and began shouting at Mrs Shortland, accusing her of setting the distances incorrectly. The instructress was struggling to keep her temper, but her voice was icily polite.

"I'm very sorry, Mrs Peters," she said, "but this is the intermediate ride, after all. All the other ponies are between fourteen and fifteen hands, to suit their riders, so I have spaced the fences accordingly. I can't move the whole lot and put everyone else wrong, just for the sake of one person. Amanda had better sit this one out, or go and join the affiliates on their bigger horses."

That didn't go down at all well with Granny, who retired to the fence, grinding her teeth and muttering darkly.

"Right," Mrs Shortland said, while we all took a breather. "Well done all of you for passing C +, but now you are working for B test and it is much more demanding. You will be expected to ride an unknown horse for the examiners, and get a reasonable performance out of it. If no one has any objections, for the last ten minutes you will swop ponies. Make sure you get one you haven't ridden before, and each give an individual display of what you can make it do."

Granny, on the sidelines, was making gobbling noises about some people having very valuable horses that shouldn't be hauled about by amateurs, but Mrs Shortland ignored her. Would you believe it—I ended up with King Kong.

I suppose it was because I had been used, all my life, to riding horses that were far too big for me, but I got on really well with the tall black horse. It didn't mean that I rode any better than Amanda, it was merely a question of having learnt, when riding work on Uncle Derry's racehorses, with my stirrups hitched up short; to use my seat, back and hands in a certain way. When it was my turn, I became totally absorbed in getting the feel of King Kong. As we trotted and cantered circles, suddenly he dropped his nose, started tracking up and lost his worried, puzzled expression.

Perhaps tact is not my strong point, but having found that I could, quite easily, adjust the length of the black horse's stride, I put him into a short, bouncy canter, and jumped him down the line of fences with no trouble at all. This time it was Mrs Shortland who called 'Bravo', while Vinny and co. split their faces grinning and Amanda gave me a long, venomous scowl. I had the nasty feeling that I'd made an enemy at the Rectory.

Having enjoyed the loan of Fred for two days running, I thought I ought to do the honourable thing and clean all his tack. The room was full of cheerfully gossiping liveries, and Cathy was telling me a long, involved story about Fred and his absent owner, but I was not really listening. It was hard to concentrate with Amanda's ramrod back, on the far side of the room, radiating waves of arctic dislike in my direction. I was saved when Liz Trent came to ask me to bed down a box for Flame. Uncle Derry had rung her to say that he would deliver my horse first thing next morning, on his way to a West Country rececourse.

The Rectory yard was dominated by the L-shaped coach house. The odd-shaped tack room was in the angle of the building, and its long, west-facing wing contained the big feed room and one enormous loose-box, where a shire horse colt was stabled. The shorter, south-facing wing, with its own private door to the tack room, was kept for the exclusive use of the Trents, but housed at the moment only Cathy's two ponies, Talisman and Squirrel. The rest of the stables were wooden loose-boxes that ran down either side of the yard to the gate arch.

I was ripping open the polythene bales and spreading shavings for Flame's bed, when Vinny came up the walkway and peered through the sliding grille door that converted the one-time Victorian stall into a loose box.

"Well I never, you are honoured," she said, and I thought, her tone was a little sharp. "Best boxes in the yard, these are, and no one but Cathy ever gets to use them."

"You know we're nearly full up at the moment," Cathy soothed. "The only spare stables we have are the two in here. It's a sort of emergency, and it won't be for long anyway."

"You try telling Granny that. She's been angling to move her precious King Kong in here, where his hugeness will have more room and be away from the riff-raff in the yard," Vinny said, sourly. "Amanda will not be best pleased to see Flame getting what she can't have!"

"Too bad," Cathy remarked, rubbing the nose of the silver-dun Welsh mare with the chocolate brown mane and tail. "Squirrel would get a stiff neck, trying to talk to something that tall!"

Squirrel, I found out, was the family favourite whose native Welsh strength would continue to carry Cathy in Mountain and Moorland classes. I hoped that Flame would treat Squirrel with the respect that, obviously, was her due, but I was more concerned by the prospect of further annoying Amanda Peters.

The unexpected preparations for Flame's arrival made me late home and, once again, I was tired and hungry. Nevertheless, I couldn't resist a visit to my yard to see how the builder was getting on. I needn't have wasted my time! A metal rubbish skip stood in the middle of the yard, but all it contained, so far, was the pile of weeds and the huge yard doors. Nothing else had been done.

I lingered in the wide gap left in the yard wall by the removal of the two doors, and enjoyed the feeling of peace in the July night. The air was as warm and soft as velvet, full of the gentle sounds and scents of a country summer. A full moon splashed silver dapples across the cobbles, its beauty making me feel deeply content. So why was I beginning to shiver?

The temperature seemed, suddenly, to have dropped and I clutched my sweater around me, shaking with cold as gooseflesh rose on my arms and neck. Then, with a sinister whisper, the wind began. The chill breeze came out of the shadows by the tack room, gathering, building, until it was hissing round the yard with menace in its breath.

The breeze grew into a gale of icy force. The old doors in the skip began to lift and fall in its power, crashing themselves into matchwood against the skip's metal sides. Trees bending over the yard wall were whipped into a frenzy, their branches thrashing, to be shredded against the stone and stripped of their whirling leaves. The noise and the force was intolerable, and I slammed my hands over my ears, trying to shut it out.

But I couldn't shut out the feelings. My nerves tingled with the sensations in the wind. They were there but not there, faint yet overpowering, intangible but piercingly real: the feelings of thrilling excitement mixed with extreme fear.

The emotion-packed wind swirled all about me until I was buffeted and breathless. Then it hurled me to one side and swept through the empty space in the yard wall, to howl away across the meadow. Suddenly the yard was once more silent and still. I was shaking uncontrollably and my teeth were chattering.

The scream came seconds later, cutting the night like a knife blade. It was high-pitched and terrified, holding nothing of excitement but a world of fear. It was a young voice screaming, to be cut short on a gurgling, ragged choke. I was running, making instinctively for the brook, my breath coming in searing gasps and my heart hammering.

It was calling me, pulling me, and I tripped and fell by the grey water, skidding into the shallows but fighting it all the time. I grasped at the tussocky grass and pulled myself clear, but I could feel to my very soul the full horror of drowning. Lying safely on the bank, I experienced the agony of being pressed down by a great weight under the airless water, until my ears sang into spiralling darkness.

I may have blacked out for a second or two, but

then my good sense took charge and I was scrambling to my feet, remembering the scream. A child, I thought, one of the noisy group of youngsters that was always playing in the lane. A child must have wandered across the paddock and fallen into the brook. Frantically, I ran up and down the bank, peering into the water, confused by the hedge shadows, moon-cast across the ripples.

The brook was shallow enough for a child to stand up in, and the current was far too weak to carry away a body, but I found nothing. Nevertheless, I knew. I was totally convinced that someone had gone into that water and not come up again. I was running once more, this time to Bridge Cottage to raise the alarm.

I'm not sure for how long the urgent confusion lasted. There were worried parents and policemen everywhere, while firemen with search-lights waded along the brook, poking long poles into the weedy banks. The village constable went from house to house, asking if anyone had lost a child or if someone was missing. No one was, and they found nothing.

I was crouched by the Aga, wrapped in a blanket but still shaking with cold and shock, when the hall clock chimed midnight. By then my mother's sympathetic comforting had changed to annoyance. She began to make caustic remarks about adolescent over-dramatics and teenagers imagining things. My father, too, was embarrassed that I'd been the cause of such a fuss for no good reason.

The village policeman spoke quietly into his radio,

drained his coffee mug and rose wearily from a kitchen chair.

"Well, we're all finished and I'll be off now, but don't you be too hard on the maid," he said, with kindness and a West Country burr in his voice. "Better we be told and 'tis a false alarm, than not say and a kiddie is hurt. 'Twas a vixen most like. They can scream to curdle the blood."

He left with my parents' apologies following him down the drive, and I was sent to bed with the distinct feeling that I was in disgrace. I lay, sleepless, on my bed all night, watching the full moon ride across my window to be swallowed by a pale dawn.

I pondered the constable's words. Fatigue can play funny tricks on the mind and I had been very tired, but I have heard a vixen call many times. Try as I might to be sensible and accept his explanation, I found no comfort in the policeman's theory. I was sure that it had been no fox that screamed by the brook that night.

FIVE

Dawn brought me the oblivion of utter exhaustion, and I overslept. I almost missed Uncle Derry. The racehorses that he trains are worth thousands of pounds and their owners expect value for his high fees, so Uncle Derry's horsebox is spectacular. Its gleaming, coach-built, luxurious length was wedged into Blind Lane, surrounded by a crowd of Rectory liveries wearing stunned expressions, when I stumbled, bleary-eyed, round the corner.

"Rachel love!" Uncle Derry swept me up in a great bear hug. "I've missed you, pet, and so has Flame."

I didn't believe the last bit for a minute. Sam, Uncle Derry's travelling head lad, was leading Flame down the ramp to the 'oohs' and 'aahs' of the onlookers. Of course, Flame was dressed for travelling in the same way as the rest of the priceless cargo: monogrammed summer sheet, leather knee and hock boots, wall to wall bandages and a poll-guard over his brass mounted headcollar. He ignored me and looked over my head, posing for his admiring public.

"Sorry I can't stop, love, we're cutting it fine to get to Exeter as it is." Uncle Derry hugged me again. "Give my love to your Mum and Dad, and look after yourself."

Sam handed me Flame's rope, and my horse deigned to recognise me and started searching my pocket for mints.

"Sure, and we all miss you too, Miss Rachel," Sam said. "I've unloaded your tack and stuff by the gate, and I wish you'd be after lettin' us in on the secret of getting Colleen to work any sense, for there's no one else who can!"

I began to feel sniffy and homesick, remembering the gangling, unco-ordinated filly from Sam's native Ireland that I had been schooling before I left home. It was just as well that the horsebox was already backing away up Blind Lane or I'd have gone with them.

The crowd in the lane closed in to get a closer look at Flame.

"Don't normally hold with spindly thoroughbreds," said fat Dot Richards, who owned a massive shire horse colt, "but this one looks rather special."

"Lovely head and unblemished legs," admired the middle-aged sisters, Enid and May Bryant, who specialised in producing show ponies.

"His colour is spectacular," breathed Eve Littleton, who show-jumped her mare, Hayley. "Can he jump?"

Liz Trent was running her hand down Flame's neck, which was about the only bit of him showing under his travelling finery.

"His colour is technically liver-chestnut, I suppose," she said, "but it hardly describes him at all. He makes Talisman look dull. Flame's coat is such a rich red, that it looks hot enough to burn your hand if you touch him!"

"It's a characteristic of his blood-line," I explained. "Red Fire, his dad, is the same. All the Reds have been the same colour for generations back."

"Not THE Red Fire," marvelled Eve Littleton, sounding awe-struck. "Red Fire the steeplechaser? I bet Flame can jump then!"

I had to admit that Flame had inherited his sire's love of jumping, and the admiring audience parted as I led him into the yard. Cathy and her mother struggled behind with my tack and kit trunk.

"What a dinky little saddle!" Cathy exclaimed, "but I bet it's uncomfortable. How on earth can you ride with such short leathers?" I couldn't think why Uncle Derry had brought my racing saddle as well as my normal one, because I rarely, if ever, used it on Flame.

"Oh, so this is the failed racehorse. A bit overdressed for a didn't run, isn't he?" Amanda's scathing voice came from King Kong's stable, and I could see her glowering expression over the half door, as I led Flame into the stable that Granny coveted in vain for the black horse. At least, I thought, Amanda hadn't called Flame sweet.

Talisman shrieked a welcome to the newcomer, from his stable at the end of the building, then set to rattling his hoof against the partition and making nickering enquiries. Little Squirrel, in the box next door, pressed her goggle-eyed face against the partition bars and assumed an expression of star-struck hero worship. Flame ignored them both. My horse stalked, unimpressed, into his new home, looking down his supercilious nose as if his neighbours were the lowest form of life.

I was too weary and depressed to enjoy Flame's first day at the Rectory. Nobody in the village could have escaped noticing the policemen, the firemen and all the fuss at Bridge Cottage the night before and, it seemed, everybody for miles around had learnt the whole story within seconds. Jokes about screams in the night flew round the Rectory yard all day, most of them good-natured and well meant, but I didn't find them funny.

Vinny said it had all been due to my subconscious wish to drown somebody, and her personal nomination would be Amanda, if it was all the same to me. Unfortunately, Amanda overheard. She glared at me with even deeper resentment, if that were possible, and called me a disgusting show-off who had made it all up to draw attention to myself.

Giving Flame peace and quiet to settle in was patently unnecessary, but a good excuse to avoid everybody. I offered to clean tack while everyone else went for a hack, and they thought I was mad. Liz Trent, who had several full liveries in the yard, greeted my idea like a gift from heaven, heaped the Bryant sisters' show tack on the table and dashed away to do her shopping.

The deserted tack room was an oasis of peace, with only Bigpuss, the stable cat, purring softly in his chair to keep me company. I've always found tack cleaning to be conducive to deep thought so, for over an hour, I cleaned and thought deeply. It didn't get me anywhere.

I remained convinced that what I had heard by the brook was neither my imagination nor the call of a vixen. I wondered if Batty Ben's fear and wild words had influenced me in some way, so that I dreamed up an atmosphere of cold dread in the stable yard and by the water. But then I remembered that first evening at Bridge Cottage, when I had run in unexplained panic from the brook, and I knew that it, whatever it was, had been reaching out to touch me long before I met Ben.

I was upset and embarrassed to be the centre of so much attention, I wished that I had never raised the alarm, yet what else could I have done? Thinking back and reliving the strong, terrifying conviction that someone had drowned, I knew I could have done nothing else.

"Rachel, quick. Come quickly!" Cathy hurtled into the tack room, dumped Talisman's saddle on its rack and rushed out again.

"Come on, slow coach!" Vinny didn't get Pearly's saddle even as far as its rack, but up-ended it on a chair. "You'll never guess who's just turned up. It's Danvers Christie-Bailey. It's really him."

"Who?" I asked.

"Danvers Christie-Bailey," Vinny repeated, impatiently. "The show jumper. Well, the ex-show jumper. He coaches people now. He coaches the British Team, even."

Rich was breathless behind Vinny. "How on earth Granny fixed it that he'd come here to teach Amanda, I can't imagine. I mean, people go begging to him, and travel miles to be taught at his place."

"Oh, do hurry up," Vinny chivied. "Amanda was booked for a lesson with Mrs Shortland, and now Granny is giving her the order of the boot. I must hear what she's saying."

We sprinted across the yard, under the gate arch and

over Blind Lane to the car park. The manege was on the left of the car park, the jumping paddock was on the right, and Amanda was sitting on the dozing, black tower of King Kong in the middle.

"You are probably fairly adequate as an instructress at Pony Club level," Granny was saying, "but Amanda has gone beyond the limits of what you can teach. It's obvious that you don't understand the needs of such a talented rider. Amanda and Ebony King are destined for great things in the showjumping world, and messing about over tiny jumps with the wrong spacing just won't do!"

Mrs Shortland was smiling and not looking at all upset, while a military-looking man, whose face was vaguely familiar to me, was standing to one side with his arms folded and his head bowed. He appeared to be studying the ground with great interest, but I could see his lips twitching. I was certain that he was struggling not to laugh.

"Dear, dear Danvers," Granny gushed on, "is such an old friend. I used to hunt with his father when dear Danvers was this high." Granny waved her hand about, somewhere at ankle level. Granny must be excessively old, I thought, or Dear Danvers had been a very stunted youth.

"Sorry to pinch your star pupil, Milly." The Great Man looked up grinning, and shook hands with Mrs Shortland. "I didn't realise it would be you. Good to see you again!"

"Hello, Danny!" Mrs Shortland gave Granny an innocent look. "Danny and I knew each other when we were this high," she said.

"And," continued Danvers Christie-Bailey, "we trained together when we were both in the junior British team. It was years ago but Milly used to knock spots off me!" Granny was speechless, and everyone else began to giggle.

Of course, when the lesson began Granny shooed us all away, which made everyone furious. We tried standing on top of the muck heap by the yard gate, but could see only King Kong's ears over the wall, and could hear nothing, except for Granny's penetrating voice saying "bravo! Amanda" every five minutes.

"I'm green, positively bright, emerald green with envy," Vinny grumbled. "What wouldn't I give for a lesson, just one teeny, weeny lesson with someone like Danvers Christie-Bailey?"

"I wouldn't get so worked up over it if I were you," Rich consoled her. "He'll have to saw at least six inches off King Kong's legs to make their combination work."

"Don't you be too sure," I said, feeling that someone ought to stick up for Amanda. "She's a very gifted rider, and more than skilled enough to come to terms with the horse, even if he is miles too big for her. Amanda can do it, but I wouldn't bet on King Kong managing much high powered showjumping. He hasn't got that sort of a jump in him. He hasn't got the scope or the brains for it either."

"Well, I hope you're right," Vinny said waspishly. "It would do her good to be taken down a peg or twelve."

"It's not her fault," I objected. "She's been Grannied, and I don't think she has a say in anything."

I groomed and fed Flame, and settled him for the

night in front of yet another admiring audience. His coat glowed under the brush and everyone continued to exclaim over its hot, red colour. All the attention and tit-bits were doing no good to Flame's modesty, that is if he ever had any. It must be genetic inheritance that makes him so aware of admiration. He may have been denied all the basking in glory after winning races that his relatives enjoy, but he's made up for it by turning showing off into an art form. Flame showed off in a disgusting manner, until I shut his door and left him to his hay net.

You know how it is when you have a sore tooth: you just can't leave it alone, you keep prodding it with a finger or pushing at it with your tongue. My stables were having the same effect on me. After last night, any other sane person would have kept well away from them, especially in the dark, but I was drawn back as if by a magnet. Like the sore tooth, I had to know if it would still hurt.

I wasn't sure what to expect, as I stepped tentatively through the gap in the wall and felt my way into the yard. Great banks of clouds had been building up all afternoon, to obscure the sunset and bring an early dusk, so that now the world was reduced to shades of grey under a black sky. The dark bulk of the stable building loomed in front of me and I stood still, waiting.

Nothing happened. I didn't know whether to be relieved or disappointed. The yard felt perfectly peaceful and friendly, with nothing out of the ordinary to feel, and nothing to see except the evidence of the builder's hard day's work. The skip was overflowing with all the rubbish from inside the building, and the dented feed bins were perched, precariously, on the top. Two new yard doors leant against the wall, beautifully carpentered, but still raw, untreated wood. I could smell linseed oil from the new putty round the stable windows.

There was no point in my waiting any longer. It was getting late and, as I reached the doorless entrance to the yard, I saw lights in the cottage window and remembered that I was hungry. Just then, the ragged clouds drifted apart to reveal the moon, and everything was flooded suddenly with silver light.

This time it hit me from behind. The freezing fury of excitement and fear crashed, like a blasting wind from hell, across the yard. It swirled and tossed me in the doorway, boiling to a crescendo of noise and unbearable emotion, until it lashed through and around me, to storm away across the meadow.

I was chilled to the marrow and shaking with fear, but I knew what to expect next. I was facing the brook when it came. The scream was deathly and followed almost at once by the tormented, gurgling choke.

It was no child, no fox, no warm, living being, it was nothing of this world that fled the yard with tragedy at its heels. Nothing visible or tangible gave that awful cry before gasping out its life under the grey water. I didn't need, this time, to call rescuers to the brook. I knew they would find nothing.

SIX

I am quite reasonable enough to admit that I may have imagined something once, but I could not accept that I had imagined exactly the same thing twice. No. It might be invisible, beyond my comprehension, but the fear that haunted my stables and the brook was not imaginary. It was horribly, undeniably real.

There, I had admitted it to myself at last. I had used the word 'haunted'. As I've said before, I do not believe in ghosts. Because of this, I had turned myself inside out, trying to be sensible and to find a rational explanation for everything. I had blamed Vinny and Ben for influencing me into finding normal things frightening, I had blamed hunger and tiredness for my feelings of nauseous dread, and I had invented a drowning child to explain the scream by the water.

I could be sensible no longer. I had no choice, now, but to face the fact that something dark and paranormal was touching my life. I could not ignore it, but neither could I live with it. I could have no peace of mind until I found out what it was and why it was there. I had never before been faced with a situation that I could not handle, and I felt helpless, desperate and very, very frightened.

I needed someone to talk to, but there was no one in Swallowbridge in whom I dared to confide. I knew that if anyone else came to me with such a ridiculous story, I would laugh in their face. I could just imagine Vinny and Rich doubling up with derision. My parents thought already that I was suffering from a bad attack of adolescent jitters, so it was no use my confiding in them, and all my old friends were miles away in Lambourn.

"What's wrong, Rachel?" Cathy's question came from Talisman's stable, where she was grovelling about in the shavings with rubber-gloved hands, mucking out his bed.

"Honestly," she went on, "this horse is the filthiest thing ever to live in a stable. I swear he dances the tango all night, on purpose to churn it all up together. Mum has christened him Poops, and refuses to have anything to do with mucking him out. Rachel, if you don't cheer up and say something, I'll scream."

I thought I'd been putting on a pretty good act of being cheerfully normal, and I was surprised by Cathy's insight, but I didn't dare tell her. I hardly knew her, and I couldn't expect her to keep my confidences from her lifelong friends. The vivaciously chattering Vinny would spread the news that I was deranged right across the county in an afternoon. I continued to brush Flame, unable to find any words.

"Look, it's O.K. if you don't want to tell me now," Cathy said. "Just remember that I'm here if you need a shoulder to cry on, and I know when to keep my mouth shut."

With little or no enthusiasm, I exercised Flame in the school, but he sensed my mood, went dead on the bit and refused to co-operate. I hoped no one had noticed my appalling display of horsemanship. I decided to take him to Bridge Cottage and turn him out in the paddock, then I could hide myself away for the rest of the day.

My heart sank when I reached the cottage and found Batty Ben standing, as usual, in the lane. It was unnerving, the way he was always there, early in the morning when I got up and late in the evening when I went to bed. I had the suspicion that he stayed there all night. I hated him.

It was not as if he did anything to frighten me and, since Dad had had a good shout at him, he never again came inside the paddock. But he would stand, unmoving, for hours on end, staring fixedly across the field at the gap in the stable yard wall. Most of the time he was silent but, if he saw a movement or heard the sounds of sawing and hammering, he would start to mutter, and then to shout about closing the doors.

I had an odd feeling about Batty Ben; I hated him but felt drawn to him. So far, I had managed to avoid him, but today he was standing right beside the gate, and I had no choice but to pass close to him.

"Good morning, Ben," I said, trying to keep the tremor out of my voice. He kept his back to me.

"You opened they doors, you shouldna' done it," he mumbled. I took a grip on myself and answered firmly.

"Never mind, Ben. What's done is done. The builder has made new doors, strong ones. He will hang them soon. I will make sure they are closed tight, then you can go away and stop worrying."

"Makes no difference. You opened they doors an' now 'tis too late. 'Tis no use all they folks and all they police lookering. They won't find un. He's gone, gone in the water."

I could feel the hair rising on the back of my neck. Ben knew something about the brook.

"What about the water, Ben? Who's gone in the water?" I stammered, then I began to shout at the old man's hostile back. "Ben, look at me. Tell me about the water, you must!"

He turned, but as he turned, his slack mouth and vacant eyes tightened into an expression of sheer horror. I was standing only a few feet behind him, and Flame was standing quietly by my side. Ben backed away until he was pressed against the hedge. He began to shake, and to make little whimpering noises like an animal in pain.

"It's alright, Ben. You needn't be frightened of Flame, he won't hurt you. But what about the water? Ben, you must tell me what you know."

Desperate to force an answer from the old man, and trying to reassure him about Flame, I led my horse a step or two nearer to Ben. Sensing an audience, even if only a pretty feeble one, Flame began to show off. He arched his neck and shook his head until his mane flew, then struck out at the road with a snaking forefoot. The effect on Ben was disastrous.

"The burning, the burning," he gasped, and all the colour left his face. He held up his hands, as if to ward us off. "It's the burning!"

"It's only his colour, Ben," I said impatiently, "that's why he's called Red Flame."

Batty Ben dropped to his knees and cowered into

the grass verge. "Burning red, that were it, burning red, and I'd forgot. They beat I till my head were dark and I couldn't remember," he mumbled.

He scrambled onto all fours and began to crawl away, then stumbled to his feet, shambling backwards, staring at Flame with wide, terror-filled eyes. He fell and struggled up again, with blood on his forehead and hands, his gaunt face awash with tears and spittle.

"The burning is out. You opened they doors, now the burning is out again. The burning and the water will take you, like they took him."

Ben's panting words reached me as he crested the rise of the little, hump-backed bridge. He tripped and fell against the stone coping, face down towards the water, and the sight of it seemed to distress him even more. He recoiled, with his arms flung across his face, and set off at a stumbling run.

For a long minute, shock held me rooted to the spot, then Flame's impatient tug at his rope brought me back to reality. I must catch up with Ben, I must find out about the water. I loosed Flame hurriedly into the paddock, forgetting to leave his headcollar on his head. He rioted away across the grass in a blurr of speed, squealing his freedom and his intention not to be caught for hours.

"Ben, wait, come back!" I ran over the bridge and down the gently descending lane on the other side. Ahead of me, the moor road to Winterford snaked its way across a landscape of sedge and mewing waterfowl. There was no one in sight. The terror of what he knew had lent wings to the old man's heels and Ben was gone, leaving me with just his threat "the burning and the water will take you".

I had thought that I knew the full meaning of fear, but I was wrong.

"Village cricket," Dad enthused. He had played for a junior county side in his youth, and had never lost his passion for the game. "Absolutely nothing like village cricket on a summer afternoon. Didn't realise that Swallowbridge has such a good team, and they keep a keg in the pavilion too!"

Mum was packing a picnic tea, but glanced up to give me a worried look.

"What's wrong, Rachel? Seen a ghost or something?" she was filling a thermos flask from the teapot, although it was obvious from Dad's expression, that the liquid refreshment served in the cricket pavilion would be more to his taste.

"Er, nothing, just tired," I said, with forced cheerfulness.

"Why not come along to the match with your father and me? An afternoon lazing in the sun will do you good." It was an appealing idea, it would give me peace and quiet to think.

Swallowbridge village cricket ground was, indeed, a peaceful place. White-clad figures were dotted across the green pitch, against the backdrop of centuries-old oak trees. The lazy murmur of spectators rose into the warm air like the hum of distant bees, interrupted every now and then by the click of leather on willow and the soft patter of applause. But, if I had hoped to get away from everyone, I was in for a disappointment.

"Owzat?" howled a familiar voice. Cathy's idiot

brother was looking unusually presentable in his white shirt and flannels, but the scarecrow head and the demon-bowler action were the same. The batsmen skied the ball and the lanky figure of Rich hurtled forward to catch it, performing an over-dramatic tumble and a couple of quite unnecessary rolls while he clutched it into his stomach. The umpire held up a finger and the spectators clapped again.

"Hello there, I'm Bob Trent. You must be the new folks from Bridge Cottage. Come along and meet everybody." Dad shook hands with Cathy's father, and was soon grinning from ear to ear across the top of a pint mug, and helping to change the numbers on the score board while he chatted. Liz Trent bustled Mum inside the pavilion to meet the other village wives, who were cutting sandwiches, and they were all soon deep in getting-to-know-you conversation. It became a very sociable afternoon that I could have done without.

My face ached from trying to smile and make small-talk, when the only thing on my mind was the vision of Batty Ben fleeing in terror, taking the burden of his unshared knowledge with him. Cathy and Vinny turned up in time for the feast of a team tea, and I forced myself to join in the chorus of congratulations that Rich and Charlie seemed to expect, then stared at my plate and tore a ham sandwich into tiny fragments. When the boys went to pad-up after tea, I slipped away and sat by myself under a tree, on the far side of the ground.

"Fixed grin, desperate eyes," Cathy remarked, flopping onto the grass beside me. "I'll go away if you'd rather."

"No, please stay," I said, surprising myself.

We sat in companionable silence for a long while, and Cathy began, with great concentration, to make a daisy chain. Then I found myself telling her everything, from my horror at the atmosphere in the old tack room, the two identical experiences of the wind and the scream and, last but by no means least, Ben's disturbing reaction when he saw Flame that morning, and his horrific prophesy of doom. It all sounded ridiculously unbelievable on a bright summer afternoon, but Cathy heard me out in unsmiling silence.

"Some people," she said slowly, her eyes on her thumb nail as it pierced a daisy stalk, "have an extra sense. You say you don't believe in ghosts, but they don't have to be blobs dancing about in white sheets goin 'woo woo', you know!" she glanced up and grinned, then became serious again.

"I think you must be psychic. No, don't make that face at me, I mean it. It's often the least likely people, the kind that think it's all a load of nonsense, the most down to earth people, who turn out to be psychic. Perhaps Ben is psychic too, and his muddled old mind has experienced something of what you felt. For heaven's sake don't let him scare you so much though, he can't possibly know what he's talking about. He's been mentally handicapped all his life, as far as I know, and never makes much sense, even when buying a pint of cider!"

Cathy's calm, practical words should have been reassuring, but my only relief came from having someone to talk to at last.

"I believe," Cathy continued, "that it's quite possible for something that has happened in the past to leave a timeless impression on a place. Especially when strongly felt emotions, or tragedy, or great fear, are involved. It's like the reverberations of a bell that go on sounding, long after the bell has been struck. People like you and, maybe, Ben can pick them up in the present."

I began to protest that I couldn't possibly be psychic. I wasn't the least bit imaginative or hyper-sensitive, and if I were at all capable of extra-sensory perception, surely I would have found it out by now!

"Not necessarily," Cathy said. "It could be that you have never before had a reason to use your psychic powers. I'm willing to bet that something very disturbing happened long ago at Bridge Cottage, so disturbing that it left behind this restless echo in time, and whatever it was would have a special meaning to you. It must have been an event that you would have felt strongly about, or that is related to experiences in your own life. That's why you in particular can hear the echo."

I thought for a moment, and then shook my head. "No I'm sure that there is a drowning involved somewhere, and I've never been near to drowning myself, I've never had a friend or a relative who has drowned either. I know you think Ben has nothing to do with it but, say he does know something and we take his words at face value, then there was a fire too. Again, I've never had any experience of a fire."

Cathy chewed on a grass stalk and stared across the cricket ground, her attention caught by a flurry of movement. Charlie had swung his bat to hook the ball and send it soaring over the boundary. The patter of applause reached us, and the distant figure of my father leapt up enthusiastically to add a six to the score board.

"Historical research," Cathy said, decisively. "That's what we need to do. We must find out absolutely everything that has happened at Bridge Cottage, your stables and by the brook—going back a long way."

"Crumbs!" I exclaimed, "that's a tall order, where on earth do we start? And we needn't bother about the cottage, I've never felt anything sinister there."

"O.K. You're the psychic, you should know. Not the cottage then."

"I'm not psychic," I almost shouted at her. "If I were we wouldn't need to research because I'd know, wouldn't I?" Cathy just laughed at me.

"We'll have to start where we can," she said, "and see what turns up. Old people who have lived in the village all their lives might know something. Old Dot Richards, for example, who keeps her shire horse at our place, she's a villager born and bred. We can quiz her too." Cathy noticed my reluctant expression. "Don't worry, we needn't tell anyone WHY we want to know. I shan't breathe a word to anybody, honest."

"I'm sure Batty Ben knows something," I insisted.

"Mm. I think that's very unlikely. But we'll find out all we can about him as well, if it will make you feel better."

"Batty Ben is incredibly old," I mused, "maybe whatever it was actually happened to him."

"Don't be daft. He can't be a ghost. He's not dead!"

I could hardly disagree with that logic.

SEVEN

If it ever came about that Cathy and I had to make our livings as research historians, then I'm afraid we would starve! After one brief day's investigating, we realised that we were going about it all the wrong way and would never find out anything, so we gave up. Asking questions was the least of our problems; the day was fraught with other difficulties.

For a start, I was adamant that no one should know why Cathy and I had developed this sudden, all-consuming curiosity about the history of Bridge Cottage stables. I remained convinced that Vinny, Rich and company would think I was mad. Unfortunately, if you try to appear casual and disinterested when asking questions, all you get are casual, disinterested replies, which are not very informative.

Another problem was the close-knit, friendly character of the Rectory Livery Stables, where everyone tends to know everybody else's business. It was incredibly difficult to talk in private or to slip away on a secret mission.

"What are you two whispering about now?" Vinny asked testily, and she gave us an odd look when we told her that we were taking some fruit and magazines to the old folks' bungalows.

"Bit sudden, isn't it, this social conscience bit?" she snapped.

"I think it's a great idea, a cheer-up visit to the oldies," Rich said. "Let's buy a box of chocs and go with them, Vin." They both looked mortally offended when we said we'd rather go alone.

We were welcomed so warmly by the warden and the pensioners at the Day Centre, that both Cathy and I felt guilty about having an ulterior motive for our visit, or, indeed, about needing a reason at all. We handed round the fruit, looked at pictures of grandchildren, played cards and chatted for over two hours, and thoroughly enjoyed ourselves.

But, as far as the fact-finding mission was concerned, it was a failure. There were absolutely no village traditions, legends or stories that had been handed down for generations about Bridge Cottage. Gathered in the room were some of the oldest inhabitants of Swallowbridge, but none of them knew even of the existence of the stables. One old man was aware that there was a building, hidden behind the high overgrown walls, but he had never known what it was.

"Oh, stables, is they?" he said "I allus wondered. When I were a tacker, we used to go fishing for minnows, in the brook upalong. We got curious once, and gave they doors a good shaking, trying to get in like, but they had a gurt strong chain and lock on. Allus been locked they have, and they buildings have never been used since I can remember."

Rather tentatively, I asked him about old Ben. It turned out that Ben, too, lived in one of the sheltered bungalows, but he had nothing to do with the other residents. They didn't like him much because of his strange ways and his aversion to soap and water, and Ben spent his days wandering the fields and footpaths, rather than socialising with the others at the Day Centre.

"Too old and gone in the head, he is, to be good company," sniffed my talkative, young, seventy-year-old friend. "Come on, let's have another game of crib before you go."

Cathy and I returned to the Rectory in time for Evening Stables, full of good intentions to visit our new friends again, but none the wiser. Rich and Vinny had gone home early, probably cross with us, I thought, but Dot Richards was still in the yard.

"No time like the present, let's tackle her now," Cathy muttered.

Dot Richards was well past middle age and immensely fat, but she had the fresh, ageless face of a countrywoman and was very active for her years and size. Her life revolved around her shire horse colt, the only thing she had left when her farmer husband died, and his land was sold to pay the debts incurred by his profitless passion for breeding the huge, gentle horses.

Dot's broad-hipped figure, in an old, tweed skirt and brogues, was a familiar sight in heavy horse show rings all over the country, where she was respected for her knowledge and skill as a producer and judge of shire horses. Her colt, known affectionately in the yard as 'the Foal', was already taller than King Kong, and Dot was standing on a crate strapping his vast neck, when we asked her about the stables at Bridge Cottage.

Her reply was depressingly familiar: "Didn't know there were any!" Then I asked her about Ben.

"Whatever do you want to know about him for?" Dot said, dismissively. "He's just the village idiot. Got worse lately too, by all accounts. I used to chat with him a bit, knows his horses he does, when you can get him to make any sense. But he's gone completely ga ga now. All he can talk about is things burning."

"Yes, we know that," I said, "but we want to find out what he did when he was young, what he was like. You've lived all your life in Swallowbridge, Dot, can you remember?"

"I don't go back that far, my girl," Dot was offended. "Anyway, he's just a newcomer here, he doesn't belong to the village at all," Dot sniffed disapprovingly. "Turned up out of the blue a few years back, he did, and got one of those old folks' bungalows as easy as pie, just because he's a bale short of a load. I won't get one that easy when my time comes, you can bet on that."

I felt a pang of disappointment; all the evidence seemed to be edging Ben right out of the picture, despite my gut feeling that he was a key figure.

"Then he's never had anything to do with Bridge Cottage, has he?" I said.

"Not that I know of. He came here from Ireland. He spent all his life working in a horse dealer's yard over there."

"But what about Bridge Cottage?" Cathy asked. "Has anything awful ever happened there? Was there a big fire, or did someone drown in the brook?"

"You girls ask some odd questions." Dot gave us a sharp look. "Always been a happy house, Bridge Cottage, full of hoards of kiddies growing up, laughing and playing. Then when they were grown up and gone, Granny Callow was left there on her own, and she sold it to some London folks as a holiday home. You should stop being so morbid. There's quite enough grief in the world as it is, without you two dreaming up more."

Dot, her expression bleak, made it clear that the conversation was at an end. She clambered ponderously down from her crate and waddled away to mix the Foal's feed. Watching her go, I felt, with piercing conviction, that the future held some great sadness for her. Deliberately, I closed my mind to the vision, hating the knowing.

I flopped into a tack room chair, while Cathy opened a tin and chopped cat food into a dish. Bigpuss wove in and out of her legs, yelling that he was starving.

"It's hopeless," I grumbled. "We're never going to find out anything without going much further back in time than people can remember, but I haven't a clue how to set about it."

"Nor have I, but I know who would."

"Who?"

"Charlie."

"Your scatter-brained brother? You must be joking. No offence meant, but he's completely daft. He'll laugh himself into a fit if he finds out why we want to know, then he'll make silly jokes and be useless."

"Trust me!" Cathy didn't seem at all put out by

my unflattering opinion of Charlie, and her smile was knowingly smug.

"I would have suggested that we ask him earlier," she said, "only I guessed what your reaction would be. I thought I'd wait until we reached a dead end, then you'd have no choice."

Bigpuss was trying to wolf down his supper and purr at the same time. The noise was almost as disgusting as the mangled, dead mouse, that the cat had brought in and left under the table as proud proof that he was earning his living. Cathy toed the remains into a piece of newspaper and, rather gingerly, transferred the parcel to the bin.

"Honestly," she assured me, "Charlie's not really an ass. He looks weird and he fools about, but it's only a cover-up—he has a very sharp mind underneath. If there's anything to find out, he won't rest until he has tracked it down."

Sighing my resignation, I had to agree to enlisting the help of Charlie Trent, but I made Cathy promise that she wouldn't mention a word to him about ghosts and hauntings. If Cathy's brother was the possessor of an incisive intelligence, I thought, then he was also a master of deception.

EIGHT

Flame loves to try something new and he thought that practising for the team showjumping was great fun. He's an intelligent horse and very quick on the uptake, so he was looking for Cathy and Talisman even while still in the air over the last jump. As clever as a cat, he turned on landing and delivered me to Cathy's side, as if to say that a fumbled baton-change would be all my fault because he couldn't get me any nearer any quicker. Cathy grabbed the baton, and Talisman sprang from a standstill to a canter, heading for the first jump. I backed Flame out of the way and the others moved forward, waiting for their turn; Rich and the Wizard next and Vinny and Pearly last, because Pearly had a mental block about standing still and hers would be the dodgiest baton change. We intended to cheat a bit by boxing her in.

Rich had explained to me the rules for the Chawton Show team jumping competition. Each member of the four-rider team would jump, in turn, one round of the fences on their own, handing the baton to the next to go. We would then form two pairs and jump the course again in team formation, two ponies in front and two ponies following, each pair keeping perfectly side by side and with a consistent distance between the pairs. We would incur penalties for any faults in our jumping or our dressing, and these would be added to our time score.

Flame knew by now that Talisman was his pair and, having obligingly jammed himself against Pearly's backside until Vinny had the baton and was safely away, he lined himself up with Cathy's pony, waiting to set off in the foursome.

Cathy and I jumped stride for stride, more as a result of Flame's watchful care than anything I did, while the over-exuberant Pearly was firmly anchored behind, next to Rich and the Wizard.

"Well done," a man's voice called from the paddock fence, and I looked up to see that Danvers Christie-Bailey had joined Mrs Shortland and was watching us.

"Especially the girl on the fizzy white mare. You've really got your hands full there, haven't you? Nicely ridden, very stylish. It makes a refreshing change to see skill and schooling used to control a goey pony, rather than a harsh bit and masses of leather!" The great man smiled warmly at Vinny, who blushed crimson to the roots of her red hair.

Amanda was waiting on King Kong in the car park, and had booked the jumping paddock for a lesson after we finished our practice. She glanced impatiently at her watch and scowled.

"If she thinks she's going to psyche us into stopping early, then she's got another think coming!" Vinny muttered. "We've got another ten minutes, so there."

"That last round was very accurate, and pretty fast too. We might just as well finish on a good note," Cathy said. "We don't want to make the ponies fed up with it."

I had made it quite clear to the others that I had no intention of pushing Amanda out of the team but, as Rich quite reasonably pointed out, Amanda was too involved with her lessons to spare time for the team, and they needed a fourth or they couldn't practise themselves. Surely, he said, I wasn't mean enough to say no on a point of principle, was I? So I hadn't much choice but to agree.

We filed out of the jumping paddock, with Granny darting round our heels like a snappish sheepdog hustling us to hurry. Vinny stopped in the gateway and, rather deliberately, took her time about raising her saddle flap and reaching down to loosen her girth a hole. I avoided Amanda's furious stare, and Danvers Christie-Bailey came over in a leisurely manner, to pat our ponies and discuss our jumping.

This was not the first time that it had happened. Poor Granny was severely shaken by the fact that Mr Christie-Bailey, ("Call me Danny, kids, please," he had said), was such a good friend of Mrs Shortland and held her in such high regard. Mrs Shortland was coaching us as a team, but Danny made a point of turning up early for Amanda's lessons, to watch and give us a few tips. He said he was enjoying being involved with the Pony Club again, and had even offered to instruct at a rally.

Granny and Amanda were speechless with fury. Granny grumbled constantly that she paid Mr Christie-

Bailey a small fortune for Amanda's lessons, and we reaped the benefit for nothing. I could see her point.

Amanda barged King Kong past Flame in the gateway and began to warm up round the outside of the jumps. Grumble or not, Granny was certainly getting full value for her money, I thought. Danny had transformed Amanda and her tall black horse into a very workmanlike combination, and Granny was already voicing ambitions that reached the heights and glittering lights of Wembley Arena itself! But I had my doubts.

I had ridden King Kong, and he had given me the same feel as the unco-ordinated, dim-witted Colleen that I had been schooling for Uncle Derry. Watching King Kong work since then hadn't improved my low opinion of his brains or scope. He might make the grade to jump a few local open classes, but I was sure that he could go no further than that. Surely Danny realised this too, but perhaps he was too much in awe of Granny to contradict her.

I was humming cheerfully as I dismounted in the yard and ran up Flame's irons. We had both enjoyed the practice, and I was proud of him.

"That's better!" Vinny grinned at me over Pearly's back. "You've had a bad attack of the mopes lately, but we didn't like to mention it. Rich said it was because you were homesick and all you needed was cheering up."

I knew that my relaxed mood was only temporary, and that my cheerful smile went no deeper than the expression on my face, but I was relieved that it had fooled Vinny. Several times over the past fortnight, she and Rich had turned up, rather diffidently, at Bridge

Cottage to invite me to parties, discos or the cinema. Each time I had gone with them reluctantly, but had ended up by enjoying myself and feeling a bit better, so I was grateful. But their well meant attempts to cheer me up resulted mainly in feelings of guilt on my part, for keeping my secret from such good friends.

The secret of the haunting preyed constantly on my mind. Despite all my good resolutions to be sensible about it, my sleep was restless with images of terror and nightmares full of cold, doom-laden wind, screams and the suffocating experience of drowning. My days were distracted by apprehensions that intruded into whatever I was doing, a constant expectation of fear that was disconcertingly without form and beyond my comprehension. Not being able to understand what I was feeling, or why, was the worst part.

I kept telling myself to calm down and stop over-reacting, especially as, for the last two weeks, my stables had been warmly and innocently fear-free. All had been still and untroubled by the brook, too. I had returned, again and again after sunset, but had heard and felt nothing. It was very odd because, with the moon in its darkest phase, the stable yard and the meadow were cloaked by the blackest of nights. They should have been far more frightening in the dark than when kindly lit by moonlight.

Despite all Cathy's assurances and Dot's information that he was a newcomer to the village, my thoughts returned constantly to Batty Ben. I was possessed by his words "the burning and the water will take you". What was it that linked the fire with the water, the stables with the brook?

There was no doubt that the link existed. I had felt the fear and the force of it, and some sixth sense told me that it hadn't gone away for good. For some reason it was quiescent, waiting, biding its time until something triggered it into being again. The longer the pause, the more jittery I became, until I felt like screaming with tension. I knew that, before long, the sane, cheerful front I tried to show to the world must crack.

If only I had some facts to work on. I had the feeling that the clues were there, on the edge of my consciousness, only just out of reach but melting like mist when I tried to grasp them. If only I knew what had happened, long ago, in the stables behind Bridge Cottage, maybe then I would understand what I was facing.

I hadn't seen Charlie for days. As she had promised, Cathy had briefed him (without mentioning anything to do with hauntings etc). She told me that he had been leaving early every morning, to do the research that she had asked for, and sometimes hadn't been returning until late in the evening. The chance of Charlie discovering anything significant seemed impossibly remote to me, but it was the only straw I had left at which to clutch.

A further worry, insignificant to me but important to my parents, was that Flame continued to live as an unpaying guest at the Rectory. Liz Trent insisted that we should think nothing of it, she loved having us and Flame was welcome for as long as we liked, but he was taking up a box in a busy livery yard, and my parents felt that we shouldn't impose on her hospitality for much longer. I dreaded having to use the stables at Bridge Cottage.

Fortunately, the builder had done what builders are apt to do: he had vanished in mid job! The renovations and repairs to the stables were finished but, as yet, no yard or stable doors were hung in place, so they were unusable. I was relieved.

"Coffee or coke?" Cathy asked, when we'd put our tack away and flopped into the battered, tack room chairs. Rich was looking for something in his locker, hurling bandages and brushes onto the floor and moaning about the ability of inanimate objects to untidy themselves when he wasn't looking.

"We really ought to get the Chawton Show entry form sorted out and sent off," he said. "The team jumping is very popular and they don't take late entries on the day."

"No," I said, firmly, "it's not fair on Amanda."

"Oh for heaven's sake," Vinny protested. "We make a brilliant foursome. She hasn't even practised with us, and can you seen King Kong's thundering long legs ever fitting in with Pearly and the Wizard? He'd be in the next county even before we'd jumped the first fence!"

"She's always done it before with you," I insisted, "she'll be very hurt if she isn't at least asked."

"Ha ha, got you there," Rich gloated. "Already asked her."

"Hardly asked! More like told her she couldn't," Cathy commented dryly.

"Well, it was her Granny's fault," Rich said, defensively, "going on the way she did after Amanda's last lesson with Danny Whatsit. She was telling everyone how Amanda had a great destiny over gigantically enormous fences, and would start with Foxhunters at the very least. So I said she wouldn't be doing any more junior classes then would she, because the jumps would be so small they would be beneath her notice and the striding set for ponies too, and Granny said no she most definitely wouldn't, so that was that!"

"Rich, you're a genius," Vinny crowed, and she started to fill in the entry form, which had emerged, dog-eared and covered in hoof-oil, from the back of Rich's locker.

"I think we ought to go to a show or two before Chawton," Cathy said, "as a warm-up and to settle the ponies. The Meadford Riding School is putting on a show this year for the first time, I don't know what it will be like, but the schedule looks O.K."

The others agreed, and we studied the schedule, arguing about which classes we should do. Rich and Vinny decided on the fourteen-two and under jumping, while Cathy and I opted for the 'rider aged sixteen years and under' jumping class rather than the Open, because the schedule didn't say how high the jumps would be, and the Open class fences might be too much for Talisman and Flame. There were Pony Club Pony, Riding Horse and Showing classes to suit all of us, so it would be a very full day.

I hadn't been to a show for ages and enjoyed the planning. It was just what I needed to take my mind off my troubles. Then, after Evening Stables, Cathy drove every other thought out of my head.

"Come up to the house before you go home," she said. "Charlie has got masses of information for us."

NINE

I kicked off my riding boots inside the back door, and padded impatiently behind Cathy, along the cool, flagged passageway to the Rectory kitchen. The big room was a homely muddle of horse rugs and bandages draped to dry, piles of horsey magazines, old whips and riding hats stacked in corners, sleeping cats sprawled on chairs and a half prepared evening meal. At one end of the long refectory table, Liz Trent, with smudges of flour on her face, was fluting the pastry on a pie, calmly oblivious to the chaos around her. A litter of kittens was shredding paper all over the floor.

"Hi Rachel, find a seat if you can!" Charlie looked up and grinned, while he pushed his mother's rolling pin to one side, and spread notebooks and files over the other end of the table.

"You've really started me on something with this," he said, casually warding off a kitten that was shinning up his leg on needle-sharp claws, in hot pursuit of more crackly paper. "I never realised that Swallowbridge had such an interesting history! I'm afraid I've been side-tracked all along the line, but somewhere in all this bumph there may be the information you want. One day, I'm going to write a proper history of Swallow-bridge, you know!"

"I looked in amazement at the piles of foolscap heaped around Charlie, every sheet covered with a clear, decisive handwriting, headings and dates under-lined and all names written in capitals.

"Where on earth did you find all this?" I asked, impressed.

"Archives, County Hall, museums, parish records, church registers, libraries," he listed, "and I nosed around and asked questions too."

"We asked questions but it didn't get us very far," Cathy commented.

"The trick is knowing the right questions to ask!" Charlie said.

"But did you find anything out about Batty Ben?" I asked, eagerly, trying to hurry things along.

"Patience, woman, I thought it was the stables you wanted to know about." Charlie peered at me from under his flopping hair, but his usual teasing grin was absent. "We are talking serious history here, so first things first." He flicked his fringe back from his face, and began turning over papers with evident enthusiasm. This was a new, serious, rather scholarly Charlie Trent that I hadn't seen before, and I was surprised. Cathy and I pulled chairs up to the table, and a dispossessed cat retreated, offended, to the top of the dresser.

"At first, I found your stables a bit of a puzzle," Charlie began. "They seem totally out of place at Bridge Cottage. They are far too grandly built to belong to a cottager. Bridge Cottage is sixteenth century, and the sort of farm labourer who would have lived in it was lucky to own a cow and a few hens, let alone a couple of horses that needed to be housed in such luxury. Then I had a good look at the stables, and realised that they are nothing like as old as the cottage, in fact, less than one hundred years old, judging by the size of the bricks. Did you know that, until 1850, there was a tax on bricks over a certain size and..."

"Oh, get on with it, Charlie," Cathy interrupted.

"No intellectual curiosity, that's your problem," Charlie muttered. "Anyway, the stables began to make sense when I found out about Lord Jasper Swayle. The Swayles have been Lords of the Manor of Swallowbridge since the Domesday Book; the village wasn't called Swallowbridge then, of course, but it gets a mention."

"Do we really have to go back to the eleventh century, if the stables are relatively modern?" Cathy grumbled.

"Alright, alright. I'll take it from the end of the first world war, when the then Lord Swayle was killed in the trenches, and his son, Jasper Swayle, inherited the estate and the title. Young Lord Jasper was a really nasty bit of work, by all accounts. He was far too young for the responsibility, as well as being arrogant, stupid and violent. All the money went to his head. He wanted to breed racehorses, point to pointers, steeplechasers or something, the kind that jump anyway. He knew absolutely nothing about horse breeding, but he was used to getting his own way. He spent money like water, building stables and buying horses and the Swayle Stud was launched, in a blaze of publicity, in 1919."

"Do you think it's because of the Swayles that so

many places round here are called Swayle something or other?" Cathy asked, curiosity at last getting the better of her.

"No doubt about it. The very first Lord Swayle built the original bridge over the brook. The local yokels couldn't get their peasant tongues round "old Lord Swayle's bridge," so the village became 'Swallow-bridge'. The nursing home, Swayle Court, was once the manor house. It has Norman bits and Elizabethan bits, and . . . ."

"Charlie, please!" I wailed. "What's all this got to do with my stables?"

"Nothing," he sighed, unhelpfully. "Sorry, back to the Swayle Stud. As I said, it was started in 1919, and I reckon that was when your stables were built. Lord Jasper Swayle kept the mares at the Manor House, and built a yard for the stallions behind Bridge Cottage. It seems an odd thing to do, but I suppose it was convenient because he employed the bloke who lived in Bridge Cottage as the stallion man. Basher Simms, the stallion man was called, and he was an even nastier piece of work than his master, young Jasper, which was probably why they got on so well together. Basher Simms was a prize-fighter in his spare time, and used to go round the markets and fairs, taking on people for a wager and pulverising them. Lord Swayle used to go along to bet on him."

"What about the stallions?" I asked, trying to edge Charlie back to the subject that interested me the most.

"Stallion. He had only one. It was a real equine aristocrat from a top-notch blood line, and Lord Swayle paid an absolute fortune for it too, far more than he could afford. That, I think, was where his troubles began."

"What troubles?" I asked.

"Lord Swayle went bankrupt in 1920."

"And?"

"And not much more. There was some kind of accident and his expensive stallion was so badly injured that he had to shoot it. Then he lost all his money, the stud was finished, end of story."

"But, it just doesn't make sense." I objected "I know *something* happened in the stables, and now you say they were built only in 1919, used hardly at all, and we know for a fact that they have been locked and unused almost ever since. It *can't* be possible that nothing ever happened there!"

"Was there a terrible fire?" Cathy asked, with relish. "Was the stallion injured in a fire at the stables?"

"No."

"Or was Lord Swayle hurt in a fire, or was he drowned?"

"No. The estate was sold to pay his creditors, and Lord Swayle ran away to India. He caused an awful scandal when he got there, by beating a native servant boy to death. He was known for his rages and violence even here in Swallowbridge."

"Could there have been a similar scandal here, that caused the stud to close so quickly and Lord Swayle to go bankrupt?" I asked, remembering Ben's obsession with beatings.

"Nothing on record that I can find."

"Are you sure there wasn't a fire?" Cathy persisted.

"No, no, no! There was no fire, no drownings, no beatings."

"But there's a burnt bit on the tack room floor," Cathy reminded us.

"I know," Charlie said, "and it's obvious what happened. Someone knocked over an oil lamp, but the flames were very quickly smothered. The stables are exactly as they were built, with no sign of fire damage at all!"

I twisted my fingers and stared down at the table in depressed silence. If Charlie had truly discovered all there was to know about the stables at Bridge Cottage, then he might just as well not have bothered. None of it seemed relevant to my problems at all. That left only Ben.

"What about Batty Ben, then?" I asked.

"I can't imagine why you want to know about him," Charlie said. "I can find no connection between him and your stables." Cathy had an 'I told you so' look, and Charlie shuffled through his papers and began to read.

"Batty Ben was born Benjamin Amos Puddy in 1899. I'm certain it was him, because I checked the name on his pension book and it's the same as in the church register of baptisms. He's the right age too."

"So he was born in Swallowbridge," I exclaimed, beginning to feel hopeful again. "He did live here, after all, he's not a newcomer!"

"Don't get too excited, he didn't hang around long," Charlie said, "and his family seemed prone to very early death! Ben was the eldest of several children who all died in infancy, except for the youngest, Jeremiah George Puddy, born 1905. In 1907, when Ben was only eight years old and his little brother just two, the

Puddy parents were buried within a month of each other. There are masses of headstones in the graveyard with 1907 on them, and one reads 'died of the great sickness', so I should think there was some kind of epidemic."

"Obviously Ben survived it," I said, "so what happened to him afterwards?"

"That I can't tell you. He seems to have vanished from the village. His younger brother, Jeremiah George, died in 1920, when he was fifteen years old. It took me ages to find him because he's not buried in the churchyard with the rest of his family, but just outside it, with only his name and the date scratched on the wall. Very strange."

"So Dot must be right about Ben working in Ireland for most of his life," Cathy said. "Perhaps he couldn't bear to stay in the village when all his family was dead."

"I tried to ask Ben questions," Charlie grinned, "but I got absolutely nowhere. The old boy certainly has a fire fixation—is that why you keep on about fires?" Cathy and I said nothing, and Charlie shrugged. "Forget him. He's quite round the bend and as dense as Mum's pastry."

Liz Trent made a face at Charlie, put her pie into the Aga and waded through the kittens to peel vegetables at the sink.

"Which gets us precisely nowhere," I gloomed.

"If you'd tell me exactly why and what you want to know," Charlie reasoned, "then perhaps I could be of more help. I feel like I'm groping about in the dark at the moment."

"Ben never mentioned any names, did he?" Cathy was thinking aloud. "I seem to remember him asking if someone or other had made you open the doors, Rachel, but the name has gone completely out of my head."

My mind was a blank too. "It can't have been Swayle," I said. "That's the sort of name that sticks in the memory."

"Not that it matters, because I'm positive that Ben has nothing to do with the goings-on at your stables," Cathy said. "Especially now that we know he went away when the stables were only just built."

"What goings-on?" Charlie asked.

"Oh, this and that. . .nothing much," I said evasively.

"There is just one other thing I could try." Charlie was beginning to look intrigued. "It's a long shot, he's probably dead by now, but worth a go."

"Who or what?" I asked without much interest.

"There was a new young curate who came to the village at about the time that Lord Jasper Swayle was setting up his stud. The curate became the vicar eventually, the Reverend Peter Threadgold. He lived here, actually in this house, the Rectory, which it really was, then. If he's still alive, and if I can track him down, he might remember something about your stables."

Charlie's expression put me in mind of an eager blood-hound that had just discovered a new trail of scent, and I hadn't the heart to tell him not to bother. So far, this investigating had led only to dead ends, and I was sure that he would be wasting his time, searching for a definitely geriatric and probably deceased vicar. I made encouraging noises, though, thanked Charlie for all his hard work and left the Trents to their supper. It was too frustrating for words.

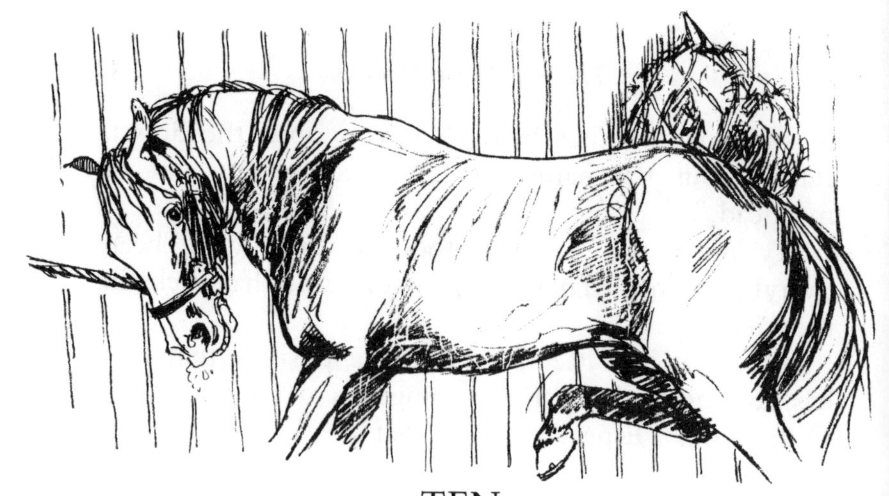

TEN

As I walked home that night, along the dark lane from the Rectory towards Lord Swayle's bridge, I had the feeling that the sleeping village was a living, breathing being, and it was mocking me. The old church, surrounded by its mossy gravestones, the historic Manor House, behind gates bearing the Swayle family crest, the time-worn stones and thatch of the ancient cottages: they all knew what had happened, but were guarding their secrets in silence. Lord Jasper Swayle, Basher Simms, the ill-fated Puddy family, even the stallion from the famous blood-line, had all walked this road before me, but the events of their lives had been swallowed by the mysterious years, to remain hidden perhaps for ever.

How could it be possible that, in finding out everything, Charlie had found out nothing? But so it seemed was the case. Either there was more to discover about the brief time in which Bridge Cottage stables had been occupied, or the answer was right under my nose and, still, I could not see it. Now, even more, I dreaded the return of the fear by the water.

The cottage was in darkness when I got home, and I remembered that my parents were at the Lark Rising Inn for the cricket club skittles evening. I took coffee and sandwiches to my room, glad of the chance to have an undisturbed think and an early night. Perhaps my head would be clearer in the morning. I was not very pleased when, shortly after ten o'clock, the phone rang.

"Rachel?" Liz Trent's voice was anxiously tense. "I think you had better come back to the Rectory straight away. Flame has colic. It's bad. I've called the vet." She hung up abruptly and I scrambled into my clothes, scribbling a note for my parents.

Flame was sweating badly, and his eyes were distressed and pain-haunted. He kept swinging his head round to stare at his flanks, then kicking violently at his stomach with a hind leg. Mrs Trent held his headcollar and talked soothingly to him, but he ignored her, locked inside his own misery. Every now and then, he would buckle at the knees, trying to get down to roll, and it was only with great difficulty that Mrs. Trent stopped him.

"I found him like this when I did my ten o'clock rounds," she said. "I don't know how long he has been like it, but he's in a bad way."

I slid back the box door and went to Flame's head. My horse recognised me and pushed his face briefly under my arm, seeking comfort, but then fought to lie down again. A swathe of headlights swept across the yard, as a car turned under the gate arch.

"That will be the vet," Mrs Trent said. "I'll go to meet him. Try to keep Flame on his feet, Rachel. He's been struggling so violently that there's the danger he'll twist his gut if he rolls."

It was a long, long night. The vet worked in grim-faced silence, my parents came and went, concerned but only in the way if they stayed, Mrs Trent was comfortingly calm and I tried to be sensible and helpful, although I was worried sick. It was shortly before dawn by the time the worst was over and Flame was resting, dopey from the pain-killing injection.

None of us could work out why Flame had had such a sudden, vicious attack of colic. He was normally robustly healthy. He was a bit of a dustbin where food was concerned, but he had never suffered from colic before, which made it all the more worrying. The vet examined my hay and hard feeds, asked questions about my feeding and watering routines, then drove away puzzled.

"You look exhausted, dear," Mrs Trent said to me. "Go home and get some sleep. I'll keep an eye on him." But I told her that I'd rather stay with Flame in his box, so she fetched me a blanket.

"If you press the green button on the tack room phone, it rings in the house," she said. "I'll leave the shaded light on in the walkway, and you can call me if you're the slightest bit worried about him."

I wrapped myself in the blanket and lay down in front of the sliding door, my cheek on my folded arms as I watched Flame, but soon tiredness made my eyelids droop and my gaze dropped to the shavings in front of me. In an instant, I was wide awake and digging in the bedding. I could so easily have missed them, had my face not been so near to the floor.

I found half a dozen of them. The brown cubes looked like pony nuts, but they were larger, darker, coarser and not pony nuts at all. Without any doubt, they were dried sugar beet cubes.

Dried sugar beet is quite a common addition to a horse's winter diet, but it is imperative that the nuts are soaked for twenty-four hours before being fed to the horse. When wet, sugar beet nuts swell to several times their own volume. If eaten dry, they do their swelling inside the horse with disastrous consequences, a severe attack of colic being one of them.

I turned the innocent-looking little nuts over in my hand. I didn't feed sugar beet to Flame in the summer, and I doubted if anyone else in the yard was using it now either. Beet nuts do not keep from one winter to the next, so I had disposed of the few I'd had left in the bottom of the sack, and I expected that everyone else would have done the same. Those beet nuts could not have got into Flame's box by accident. Someone had put them there, deliberately to harm him, and it was a frightening thought.

I let myself quietly out of Flame's stable and crossed the yard to the other wing of the coach house. I felt my way along the dark walkway, past the Foal's loose-box to the feed store, where I closed its door behind me before putting on the light. The wide room had once housed carriages and coaches, but now its walls were lined with square, metal feed bins, each with the name of a livery chalked on the top and a metal hasp to take a padlock. Fortunately, no one ever bothered to lock their bin, because the Rectory yard was not the sort of place where things went missing.

I began my search, feeling a bit like Charlie playing detective, but there was no fun in this investigation. As

I had expected, no one had the slightest trace of sugar beet in their feed bin. Except for one. The red and white plastic sack was practically empty, screwed up right at the bottom, but unmistakable. The name chalked on the bin lid was 'Amanda Peters'.

I returned to Flame's box and slumped down in the corner, my head on my knees. How could anyone be so soured by hatred to want to harm my horse, any horse, to risk killing him even? It was unbelievably horrible, disgusting, terrifying. I was aware that I had upset Amanda by being able to jump King Kong at the rally when she had failed, but she had proved by now that she was perfectly capable of jumping him herself. I had worried that I had put her nose out of joint by elbowing her out of the Rectory team, but her sights were set on higher goals and she hadn't appeared to mind. I knew that she resented the fact that Danvers Christie-Bailey gave our team so much of his time and attention, but that was altogether too petty a reason for hurting my horse. I could not believe it possible for anyone to be so eaten up by jealousy that they would do such a thing, especially without giving anyone any indication of their tormented state of mind.

Maybe I was wrong. After all, I hadn't any real proof. Just because Amanda was the only person in the yard to have sugar beet nuts in her feed bin, didn't mean that she had deliberately fed some to Flame, who is greedy fool enough to try anything he is offered. But, instinct told me, that was exactly what had happened.

There was nothing I could do about it. If I went running to Mrs Trent with wild accusations, I had no proof to back them up, and it would cause another major fuss. I couldn't cope with that, on top of everything else.

What if Amanda tried again to get at Flame? I would have to watch him every minute of the day, arrive at the yard before Amanda every morning and stay until she'd gone home every night. I must make sure that Flame spent as much time as possible in the paddock at Bridge Cottage, beyond Amanda's reach and safely out of harm's way.

As much as I hated the idea of having to use the stables at Bridge Cottage, it was now a matter of extreme urgency that I move Flame there as soon as possible. Dad had been so immersed in his work, that he had forgotten about the vanished builder and the unfinished repairs to my stables. Deliberately, I had not reminded him, hoping to extend the delay. Now I must decide which frightened me more: the idea of using Bridge Cottage stables or the possibility of Flame being hurt again.

I forgot that I was meant to be sensible. I put my hands over my face and cried some very childish tears.

ELEVEN

The fistful of rosettes that I won at Meadford Show brought me no joy at all. I was in agreement with most other riders on the show ground, that the whole thing was a waste of time and we wished we hadn't taken the trouble to go to it. It turned out to be a very amateurish affair, run by an inexperiened committee in the field of a slummy, substandard riding school.

The only satisfied people on the show ground were the hoards of children who appeared to be sharing the ribby, scarecrow ponies that belonged to the riding school. They kept up a constant screaming and yelling, galloping the legs off the poor little creatures between classes, arguing over whose turn it was to ride and showing off. I suppose the ponies were used to being treated so thoughtlessly, to being hauled in the mouth, kicked and whacked by amateurs, but I found it very sad to watch.

The jumps were tiny, consisting mainly of rusted oil drums and flaking poles, the courses were undemanding and the showing judges hadn't a clue what they were doing. The Riding Horse judge was far more impressed by Flame's flashy colour than by our presentation and way of going, so that winning the class was nothing to be proud of. But that wasn't what I minded so much. My main discomfort was that, every time the tannoy squawked 'and in first place Rachel Downing riding Red Flame', I felt — without even seeing her — Amanda's waves of jealousy, scorching towards me across the show ground.

Amanda had come to the show to do just the one class, the Open Show Jumping, which was the last class of the day. I couldn't understand why she had turned up so early, when she had her own trailer and didn't need a lift in the Rectory lorry. King Kong stalked round the ring-sides looking vastly out of place, with all the screaming kids on their scruffy little ponies milling round his legs like ants.

Amanda looked pale and ill. I couldn't believe that she was sick with nerves on her first outing with King Kong, so put it down to the fact that she was sick of me. If so, why didn't she just keep out of my way? Whenever I turned round, there she was, her expression grim and her mouth half open, as if she were about to say something.

Flame had shrugged off his colic attack with the careless ease of his robust good health and was fighting fit. I was the exhausted one, after three days of watching Amanda like a hawk and becoming paranoid about guarding Flame. I hadn't dared tell anyone of my suspicions about Amanda feeding him sugar beet and, once again, I felt alone with my troubles and lonely. Fortunately, Cathy and the others were too preoccupied with the preparations for Winterford Show to notice that I was moping again.

"It's embarrassing, isn't it?" Vinny didn't sound the least bit embarrassed. "A Rectory whitewash! How many cups and rosettes have we won between us?"

"Most of them I should think," Rich said. "Except for the games. Quite a clean-up."

"Well, I don't think it's anything to crow about," Cathy protested. "The embarrassing thing was the size of the jumps. Honestly, Talisman thought they were trotting poles. I can't think why we didn't scratch and do the Open."

"Everyone is grumbling," Vinny reported, "and the Winterford Equestrian Centre mob loaded their horses straight back into the box, and went home without competing at all."

"That's what we should have done," Cathy said, but the others shouted her down.

"After all, a cup's a cup," Rich said, "and there was a decent bit of opposition here and there." But Cathy called him a rotten little pot-hunter.

We were unpicking the ponies' plaits beside the lorry, and trying to ignore a riot in the games ring, when Eve Littleton joined us. She leaned down from Hayley's back and dumped another cup on the ramp.

"You never won the Open Jumping, did you?" Vinny exclaimed.

"I did," Eve grinned, "but nothing to get excited about. They put the fences up to three footish, but it was a silly little course, and it boiled down to which horse could scuttle round fastest."

"But that means you beat Amanda and King Kong!"

Vinny's eyes were alight with devilish glee. "And this was meant to be the stars' great debut, the first unveiling when they would dazzle us peasants with their brilliance."

"Afraid the stars didn't shine very brightly today." Eve threw a sweat rug over Hayley's back and fed the mare a mint. "I think the King was too high up to see the little jumps. He tripped over most of them. Didn't even get through to the jump-off."

"Oh dear, Granny will be furious!" Cathy predicted.

It wasn't Granny that I was worried about. Amanda would be boiling mad too, and that boded ill for Flame. I had dithered between my fear of Amanda and my hatred of my stables for quite long enough. Now my mind was made up: I must, must, must move my horse away from the Rectory Stables as soon as possible.

If anyone thought I was odd, they were kind enough not to say so. The last few days had been very hot and the flies were a torment to the horses, so most of the liveries were leaving their ponies in the cool shade of their stables during the day, and turning them out at night. There was no way I dared to leave Flame in his box at the Rectory all day, unless I was going to be there too. If I was going back to Bridge Cottage, then Flame had to come with me. The poor horse suffered a very 'now I'm in, now I'm out' existence, but he was philosophical about it.

The one brief phone call had been enough to summon the builder, unapologetic and unrepentant, and only a day's work saw my stables ready for occupation. Before the final coat of paint was dry on the stable doors, I was leading Flame down the lane to Bridge Cottage. The double yard doors looked very impressive, varnished and studded with the original, ornate bosses, and I had left one of them wide open, so that Flame could walk straight into the yard. But we never got as far as the doors!

Half way up the path behind Bridge Cottage, Flame began to hesitate and jib. Two strides later he propped violently, digging in his front toes, then he tried to swing away from the doors.

"Silly boy," I said, patting him reassuringly. "Walk on." I tugged at his headcollar and flicked the rope's end at his flanks behind me. Flame rolled his eyes and flattened his ears, then sat back on his hocks and half reared, something he'd never done before.

I couldn't understand it. Flame was far too conceited and sure of himself to suffer from silly fears and fancies. Unknown places had never bothered him before. After all, he had waltzed into the Rectory yard as if he owned the place, and had more or less taken over before he'd had a chance to look around.

"You idiot," I scolded. "That door is wide enough to drive a bus through, but I'll open the other one as well, if it will make you feel any better about it."

I dropped Flame's lead rope on the ground, which he has been trained to understand as the order 'stand still where you are', a command that he always obeys.

Promptly, he galloped to the far side of the field with his rope flying behind him. When he reached the far hedge, he spun round to watch me, giving short, barking snorts, his head high and his tail kinked over his quarters.

I opened the other door, so that the entrance to the yard was wide and inviting, and then spent ten minutes trailing after my horse before I caught him. Flame fought me every step of the way back towards the stables, and he wasn't putting on an act. His ears were plastered against his skull, his eyes were white-ringed with terror and sweat poured from his neck and flanks.

I battled with him for over half an hour, but he refused to go anywhere near the doors. In the end, he began to tremble all over, shaking as if in a high fever, and I knew I was beaten. I would have to take Flame back to the Rectory after all.

It was not Flame that I led down the lane: it was a fear-crazed stranger. He was panic-stricken, plunging, careless of barging into me and trampling on my feet. I could hardly hold him. Then I remembered King Kong, caught by his trailing reins on the bridleway and only feet away from my stable yard. He too had been going out of his mind with fright. He too had behaved like a maniac all the way back to the Rectory.

At the time, I had thought that the black horse was merely another highly strung idiot that had been spooked by the crash of the falling door. I knew him now for the dozy, unflappable creature that he was. There could be only one explanation: both King Kong and Flame had sensed something unnatural and totally terrifying about the stables at Bridge Cottage.

I was right. Although the fear had not made itself manifest for over two weeks, it was still there, waiting for me. I felt cold with the dread of it.

Flame's refusal to go anywhere near my yard presented me with yet another dilemma. What on earth was I going to tell my father? Our landlord had paid some of the expenses, but the renovation of the stables had cost Dad a lot of money too. He had done it just for me, so that I could have Flame with me for one short year in Swallowbridge, but now I would never be able to use the stables. Dad would be furious, how was I going to explain it to him, and how could I stay indefinitely as an unpaying guest of Liz Trent?

I didn't return to the Rectory straight away, but walked Flame round the lanes until his breathing had slowed to normal, he had stopped sweating and was calm and dry again. I pondered my problems: a haunting, Amanda and a homeless horse, and all three of them still seemed insolubly serious when I got back to the Trents' yard.

Cathy was running down Blind Lane as I turned the corner, with Charlie mooching along behind her, his hands in his pockets.

"There you are at last," she called. "I've been dying to tell you all afternoon, and no one knew where you were."

She followed me into Flame's stable, hopping from foot to foot with impatient excitement.

"Hurry up, Charlie, come and tell Rachel."

Charlie was eyeing one of his mother's hens out in the yard, and he picked up a rolled tail bandage from the walkway windowsill. The bird was minding her own business, innocently absorbed in murdering a worm under the water trough. Charlie demon-bowled the bandage and hit the hen, fair and square under her tail, sending her squawking and flapping across the cobbles. Cathy was too excited to protest over the fate of Talisman's tail bandage.

Charlie ambled back into the building. "If somebody would be kind enough to tell me what this is all about, then perhaps I could understand why you are getting so worked up over it!" he said.

"Just tell her, Charlie," Cathy fretted.

"I've traced the Reverend Peter Threadgold."

"Go on, tell her the important bit."

"I don't know which is the important bit," Charlie sighed. "Anyway, he's still alive and kicking, and lives with his married granddaughter in Tenby, in Wales. He's very old, but his mind is still sharp and his memory as clear as crystal. He remembers Lord Swayle and the stud and Ben, the lot. I talked to his granddaughter on the phone this morning."

"Charlie!" Immediately I was all ears. "So what did he tell you?"

"That's the problem. I wasn't able to speak to the vicar himself because he's profoundly deaf, has been for years, poor old boy. He can lip read perfectly well, so his granddaughter was able to relay my questions to him, but it still didn't work very well and was taking far too long on Dad's phone bill. The only way of getting the complete story out of him is to talk to him face to face."

"Oh *no*! But that's impossible!" My bitter disappointment must have come across in my voice because Charlie looked at me in concern.

"It means a lot to you, doesn't it?" he said. "If it's really that important, I'm quite happy to go to Tenby to talk to him. I've already had a word with our wicket keeper, Mike. He drives for Chawton Haulage Company and does a regular trip into Wales. He'll give me a lift and I can stay at a youth hostel, so it won't cost an arm and a leg."

"Do you mean it? Would you really do that?" I felt guilty about asking him to give up part of his precious summer holiday, but I was desperate.

"No problem," he said airily, then became serious. "But there is absolutely no point in my going unless I know why. I might ask all the wrong questions, then it would be a wasted journey."

He was right. I was beginning to find out that Charlie was almost always right, and I should have trusted him more in the first place. I leaned my face into Flame's mane for a long minute, then decided to tell him the whole story. It came haltingly at first and then in a flood, with Cathy chipping in to prompt me over details and to confirm the events with which she had been involved.

"Well, I'll be . . . well, I don't know what to say!" Charlie subsided onto the floor and slumped his back against Flame's door. "If I didn't have you down as a sensible, level-headed girl, I wouldn't believe a word of it! It puts a whole new complexion on everything."

Flame's refusal to go anywhere near the stable yard at Bridge Cottage, and my theory about what had terrified King Kong on the bridleway, was news to Cathy. We sat on the shavings, beside Charlie, and went over it again, while Flame, wondering what it was all about, rested his head on my shoulder and gazed enquiringly at the three of us.

Confessions must have been in the air because, while Charlie digested my story in stunned silence, I found myself blurting out my suspicions about Amanda and Flame's colic. Cathy was appalled: shocked and furious because I'd told no one.

"You'll just have to tell Mum," she gasped. "It's the most diabolical thing I've ever heard."

"No," I said firmly, "It would cause too much trouble and ill-feeling. Besides which, I have no proof that it was Amanda who fed sugar beet to Flame."

"Crumbs, but you're stubborn," Cathy complained. "You spend your life saying 'definitely no this' and 'absolutely not that', and it's beginning to get on my nerves."

"Well, I mean it!"

"But," Charlie interrupted, "just say something awful happened once, at your stables, so that now they really are haunted, how is finding out what it was going to help? It's not going to solve any of your problems, as far as I can see. Knowing *why* Flame won't go near the yard is not going, miraculously, to change his mind, nor will it make the screaming business go away."

"But it *will*, I'm sure of it!" I was feeling an overpowering conviction for the first time. "I don't know why, but it *will*. I'm *certain* that the answer will come, that I'll know what to do about it, just as soon as I know what actually *happened*."

"She's psychic," Cathy said.

"No I'm NOT," I insisted. Flame found the atmosphere altogether too intense for comfort, and retreated from my shoulder to start work on his hay net.

"Calm down, girls!" The old twinkle had returned to Charlie's eye. "Just leave it to Uncle Charles. Cathy will help you to guard Flame and I'll get to Tenby as fast as I can. I'll produce the facts, and Rachel can work the psychic miracle!"

I didn't argue. I rather hoped that, as usual, he was right.

TWELVE

There was a strained, unpleasant atmosphere in the Rectory yard all the next day.

"I can't think what's got into you kids," Eve Littleton remarked. "You usually get on so well together."

"Some petty, teenage squabble I expect," Dot Richards grunted. "They need their heads knocking together."

"One of us ought to do it then, and bring them to their senses," the Bryant sisters agreed.

And Amanda drifted about aimlessly, white-faced and red-eyed. She seemed to be following me.

It began first thing in the morning, when the liveries were making a clatter in the yard, feeding and mucking out their horses. Charlie stomped across the cobbles, looking more outlandish than ever in his enormous army boots, patched and faded jeans and a crumpled, very second-hand old mac. He had a rucksack on his back, and a rolled sleeping bag bobbed behind his shaggy head.

"Where on earth are you going dressed like that? A

tramp's convention perhaps?" Vinny jeered over Pearly's stable door.

"You never said you were going away!" Rich accused.

"Sorry, in a hurry, can't stop," Charlie called, and he herded Cathy and me into Flame's stable.

"O.K. be like that then, don't tell us," Vinny yelled after him, and she and Rich looked offended.

"Mike's picking me up in half an hour at Meadford Cross," Charlie told us, "so I'd better get a move on. I've written down the vicar's telephone number and address, and the phone number of the youth hostel where I'll be staying. Let me know if you find out anything new, or if anything else happens in the spook department." He handed me a slip of paper. "It may be several days before Mike has another load for Wales, so I don't know when I'll be back."

"Ring Bridge Cottage and reverse the charge if you have anything to report," I said, "I'll go mad if I have to wait that long to know. And have you got enough money? I haven't had time to go to the Post Office, but I borrowed this off Dad." I gave him a couple of folded notes.

"Thanks. A few square meals wouldn't go amiss, and I expect I'll have to treat Mike to a lorry driver's grease feast en route! Bye then."

"Good luck!" Cathy and I called after him, and Rich looked furious when Charlie tramped under the gate arch without stopping to talk.

"Where's he gone then?" Vinny demanded.

"And when's he coming back?" Rich asked. Cathy was obviously uncomfortable, not being able to tell her friends without breaking her promise to me.

"He'll be gone three or four days probably," I said in a suitably vague tone. "Goodness knows where."

Vinny wasn't impressed. "I never thought I'd see the day when you'd keep petty little secrets from me, Cathy Trent," she stormed.

"I've been wondering why you're always going into a huddle with Rachel, whispering and avoiding us. I suppose Charlie's in on it too!"

"And that means he'll miss the village cricket league match," Rich ranted, "and he never said anything to anybody. Just pushed off without a word and let us down. The rotten, thoughtless pig!"

"It isn't like that honestly Rich. He's helping me out of a mess I'm in and it's very important." I tried to smooth things but Rich just looked sour. "I'll tell you everything as soon as I can." I promised "Why not ask my Dad to fill in for the match, he was in a junior county side years ago."

Rich looked slightly mollified. "Charlie's never been one for dirty tricks before," he said, "'spose we ought to give him the benefit of the doubt now. Is your Dad a batsman or a bowlet?"

"Sorry, haven't a clue. The one who throws things, I think."

"Spinner or fast?"

"Heavens, I don't know, ask him."

The atmosphere remained a bit cool though all morning, except for Vinny's rejoicing that something seemed to have taken the wind out of Amanda's sails. Poor Amanda looked dreadful, as if she hadn't slept for a week and had cried herself to a standstill. At coffee time, everyone was agog with interest when Granny's

Range Rover turned into Blind Lane, towing her trailer.

Granny ignored everyone as she stalked across the yard to King Kong's stable, and she looked straight through Amanda as if she didn't exist. In no time at all, she had a set of travelling bandages on the black horse's legs and was hustling him up the ramp of the trailer. She slammed the tail-gate and climbed into the driver's seat, without saying a word to her granddaughter, then Granny and Ebony King were gone.

"Wow, I smell a real family bust-up chez Peters!" Rich said, "I suppose it's yet another secret that nobody will tell me."

"I've had enough of this. They can please themselves, see if I care." Vinny declared. "Come on, Rich, let's go for a ride, just the two of us," and she flounced away. Rich shrugged and followed her.

"I'm sorry, Cathy." I said sadly, "I seem to have spoiled everything since I arrived, and now I'm causing trouble between you and your friends."

"Don't worry," Cathy laughed. "Vinny's inclined to have a bit of a flare-up every now and then, but it's never serious. There's no better friend to have than Vinny when things get tough, and she'll probably turn herself inside out being sorry tomorrow." I hoped Cathy was right.

The wraith-like Amanda was bothering me. All the time that I was strapping Flame, she hovered about at the end of the walkway but, if I put my head round Flame's stable door, she ducked out of sight. Obviously something awful had happened in her life and, if I hadn't had so many things going on in my own, I might have felt sympathetic. As it was, I just wished that the ground would open up and swallow her, and so leave me with one less problem.

I rode Flame for an hour in the manege, losing myself in the pleasure of working through a dressage test. It made both Flame and me concentrate so hard that we could ignore Amanda, who was hanging about by the school gate. As I left the arena, she seemed about to say something, but I gave her such a loathing stare that she scuttled away like a frightened rabbit. It was a petty victory, but it made me feel better.

"When you turn Flame out, I'll walk with you down to Bridge Cottage," Cathy said. "We ought to check round your stable yard. You never know, it might have been something quite simple that put him off going in, a pile of rubbish, anything."

I had loved that little stable yard, the first time I saw it, even though it was overgrown with weeds and almost derelict. I hated it now, despite its spick and span appearance. The stable and tack room doors were painted glossy white, with the original, ornate hinges and catches picked out in black. I would have forgiven the tardy builder everything for the beautifully scripted name plate, 'Red Flame', fixed to one of the stable doors, were it not for the fact that I knew Red Flame would refuse even to cross the threshold.

The weedless cobbles were swept clean, the stone trough had been scraped of its moss and the burnished pump gushed clear water within three swings of its handle. The rubbish skip had gone and there was nothing else in the yard.

"These new doors are magnificent, he's copied the old ones exactly, even re-used the iron bosses." Cathy ran her hand admiringly over the richly grained wood. "And he's cleaned up the carvings on the stone pillars too—a shield with something animally in the middle. Look, it's the Swayle family crest!"

"It's horrible," I said.

"It's not, it's beautiful, just as it was when it was built, and it proves that Charlie was right. Lord Swayle built it especially for his stallion. Oh, I see what you mean."

Cathy withdrew her fingers hastily from the motto carved beneath the shield. It read 'My spite defies time'.

"But there's nothing here that could possibly have frightened Flame," Cathy said, as she walked into the yard. "Perhaps the smell of new paint, but even that's nearly gone." She wandered about, looking over the stable doors and peering into the tack room.

"This is smart. New everything, but he's left a heap of junk on the floor. I wonder why?"

"He told Mum there was some stuff we might want to keep, that must be it."

Hesitantly, I followed Cathy into the room at the end of the building, dreading to meet again the foetid smell of long ago violence and hate, but it was gone, banished by the busy builder. Relieved but without interest, I examined the new feed bins along one wall, the restored, wrought iron saddle racks along the other and the row of useful cupboards and shelves.

The afternoon sun was slanting through the window in the back wall, and catching dancing motes of dust in its beam. Once upon a time, I would have given the earth for a little palace like this, just for Flame and myself, but now the place was only a burden, a big problem that I had to explain to Dad. Cathy was kneeling on the floor, clanking about in the heap of rubbish.

"No way is this junk," she said, holding up a square, black object with a pointed end and bits of glass round the sides. "This is a brass carriage lamp, well worth cleaning up." She started rooting again. "Old snaffle bits, horse brasses, I wonder how they got here, stallions don't wear horse brasses. Another carriage lamp, and what's this?"

Cathy was silent for a long minute, but I was staring out of the window and paying her no attention.

"Rachel," she said eventually, in a tight little voice, "I've been wrong all along. Completely on the wrong track!" She was holding an oblong of wood and looking as if it had just bitten her.

"I'd bet my life," she said, "that this is the name plate off the stable door of Lord Swayle's famous blood-line stallion, and it's a real shaker." She turned it round and held it up to me, and I felt as if my heart had stopped.

The carving was intricate and beautifully done, with 'The Swayle Stud' in flowing, flowery letters across the top. In big, bold capitals underneath, was cut the name

'BURNING RED'.

"Ben knew all along," Cathy whispered. "We just misunderstood what he was trying to say."

"There was no fire. 'The burning' that he kept on about was a horse, the stallion called 'Burning Red'," I gasped.

"And," Cathy hurried on, "when he said 'the burning is out', he didn't mean that a fire had been put out, he meant that Burning Red was out, out of his stable, out of the yard. Someone must have opened the doors and the stallion escaped, and then he had an accident and had to be shot."

"Ben opened the doors," I remembered suddenly.

"He said someone made him open the doors and beat him because of it."

"I was wrong, Rachel, so wrong. I'm sorry. I was so sure that Ben couldn't possibly have had anything to do with it, but he must have been there, he must have seen it all."

I took the all-important piece of wood from Cathy's hands and gazed at it, wishing it could speak.

"It makes no difference," I said. "Ben can no more tell us than can this block of wood. Even Charlie couldn't make head nor tail of Ben's ramblings. We may have another piece of the puzzle, but it leads only to another dead end."

"That's where you're wrong!" Cathy scrambled to her feet, her eyes alight with excitement. "Don't you see?" You don't call a horse Burning Red without a good reason, and Ben was scared half to death when he saw Flame. Perhaps the stallion was the same colour as Flame, perhaps Flame looks just like Burning Red. Perhaps they are related, way, way back in the bloodline. You must get in touch with your racehorse training uncle at once!"

"Why?"

"Because, you slow-witted girl, he'll have all the stud books, or know where to get hold of them. Ask him to find out everything he can about the stallion Burning Red, it may well give us a lead!"

I shook my head doubtfully. It was unlikely that the stud records or form books would contain the kind of information we were seeking.

"It still doesn't explain the scream," I said. "It was a human being that I heard screaming and drowning in the brook, not a horse. The stallion didn't drown, he was shot."

"Oh don't be so defeatist, it's not like you," Cathy said, briskly. "I'm going straight home to phone the youth hostel and see if Charlie has arrived yet. He must be told. You must contact your uncle as soon as possible. Who knows, we may even learn enough of the truth to jog Ben's memory into making sense."

Cathy had a point, and I hurried after her out of the yard. But I couldn't share her optimism. Just holding the name plate, imagining the soft muzzle that must have touched it every time Burning Red looked over his door, seeing in my mind's eye the noble horse that may have looked like Flame and who met such a tragic end, had given me a bad feeling.

"I really don't know what's got into you over the past few weeks, Rachel," Mum said. "You spend every evening moping about on your own. Your father and I see hardly anything of you. I do hope you're not going through one of those moody teenager phases or whatever." She put the mug of hot chocolate on my bedside table and kissed me goodnight.

"Do try to perk up a bit, dear," she said as she left the room.

Uncle Derry had been in a hurry to go out when I rang him, so we could not talk for long. He said that he would be glad to help, but could not think why I wanted to know every last detail he could discover about a stallion that had been dead for over seventy years. I spent the rest of the evening in my room, writing down everything that I had discovered so far about my stables. But, if there was some connection, some clue that I had missed, it remained hidden. I found it hard to concentrate, because the name Burning Red kept going over and over in my head, beating in my brain.

I could hear the murmur of my parents' voices in their bedroom, then silence, but I knew that I would not be able to sleep. I switched off my light and opened wide the low, crooked window. My room was filled with the warm, sweetly scented night air, and I knelt by the windowsill, my head on my folded arms, and peered into the darkness. Somewhere in the distance a dog barked, and from Trickett's Wood came the call of a hunting owl. I think I must have fallen into a doze.

The scream tore through me with shock waves of terror.

For a moment I was confused: had I been awake, or was it yet another bad dream? An angry, red moon rode high in the sky, leering from behind its muffling of dark clouds. It was not yet at the full, but it gave sufficient light to cast dismal shadows and reveal the landscape under its lurid glow.

As I gazed across the paddock towards the brook, I felt again the compelling pull of the water. Even as the last echo of the scream faded into the night, cold fear washed up from the meadow and swamped me in its icy depths. It had come back.

I retreated from the window to my bed and curled against the headboard, my teeth chattering. Not only had it come back, as I had known it would, but it was no longer content to wait for me by the water. Now it was seeking me out, reaching to find me even in the safety of my own room.

Why? Why had it waited for so long? What had happened on this night in particular to give, once again, the long drowned a voice, and the long dead the power to touch me? Then the answer came to me.

It was the moon. The fear stalked only on moonlit nights. The tragedy had been a companion of the moon.

THIRTEEN

The next morning relationships in the Rectory yard had thawed completely back to normal. Rich and Vinny were waiting for me when I arrived, both shuffling their feet and looking embarrassed. Rich was self-consciously clutching a bunch of roses which he thrust at me. Funnily enough, the blooms were exactly the same shade of salmon-pink as those on the prized and cherished bushes in Mrs Trent's front garden.

"I'm sorry," Vinny said. "It was beastly of me to get so ratty with you."

"I'm sorry too," Rich joined in. "If you're in some sort of bother, then I'm glad Charlie is helping you. It's none of our business, unless you want to tell us."

"You know we'd do anything to help you too, any time," Vinny said. "It was very thoughtless and selfish of us to add to your troubles by being so childish."

I was grateful and thanked them. One day, when it was all over, I would tell them. I was too tired now, after my sleepless night, to launch into yet another long, unbelievable explanation.

Amanda hurried past us, up the coach house walkway towards the tack room. She looked, if it were possible, even worse than she had the day before, and she kept her head bent, avoiding our eyes.

"What are you doing here, seeing as you haven't got a horse any more?" It hadn't taken Vinny long to cover up her soft centre and get the snap back into her voice. Amanda mumbled something about clearing her locker, and vanished through the door at the end of the corridor.

"Now, if anyone is desperately in need of help, it's Amanda the Miserable!" Rich said. "I've never seen her looking so down. I vote we let bygones be bygones and give her a bit of sympathy."

"Forget it," Cathy said, coldly. "She deserves a dose of grief."

Vinny and Rich looked amazed, and I shot Cathy a warning glance, crossing my fingers that she wouldn't mention sugar beet.

"It's unlike you, Cathy, to be vindictive. You're usually the one who loves the whole world. Sorting people out is my job," Vinny said.

"I smell another Cathy and Rachel secret, judging by their expressions. No, no, sorry. I'm not getting at you, honest." Rich was worried that he'd upset us again, and we assured him that he hadn't.

The next day was the long awaited day of the Chawton Show and the much practised for team jumping competition. To keep jumping the ponies would only make them stale, so we did no more than ten minutes' baton changing practice, then exercised them across the Rectory fields in our formation of two pairs.

Horses are very sensitive to mood and atmosphere, and our ponies quickly picked up the vibrations of excitement in the air. Vinny had a hard time stopping Pearly from fizzing over altogether, while Flame and Talisman opted for synchronised piaffeing by way of letting off steam. The Wizard had his work cut out carrying his overgrown rider, but still managed an explosive rodeo display that failed to dislodge Rich only because he could wrap his long legs right under the pony's stomach.

Rich told us sadly that this would be his last show with the Wizard. His mother had found the ideal horse for him, a sixteen hand, cobby, chestnut gelding, aptly called Mr Big. His new horse would be arriving at the Rectory just as soon as a new owner could be found for the Wizard. The news effectively put a damper on things, and we spent the rest of our ride trying to think of a suitable loan home in the Pony Club, so the Wizard wouldn't have to be sold.

The afternoon was taken up with washing tails, grooming till our arms ached and cleaning our tack. Cathy was determined that the Rectory team should be immaculately turned out. It had become a point of honour for her that her mother's livery yard showed up well beside all the other teams from livery yards, riding schools and equestrian centres all over the county. None of our tweed jackets matched each other, so Cathy insisted that we wear black jackets and white shirts.

"'Spose you expect us to wear thumping great bouquets of flowers stuffed in our button holes as well," Rich grumbled.

"No. Pony Club ties and badges are much more suitable," Cathy said, momentarily losing her sense of humour. Then she cleaned Rich's tack all over again for him because, as she explained to me, the grime-encrusted state of his tack was legendary amongst Pony Club instructors, and he'd never yet managed to do the job properly.

I thought I was the last person to leave the yard that night but, as I came up the coach house walkway after locking the tack room, I glanced across to the other building and was appalled to see Amanda, standing outside Flame's box. I sprinted across the corner of the yard, elbowed past her and slammed my hand over the stable door bolt.

"Go away," I growled between clenched teeth.

"You know, don't you?" she said.

"Yes, I flaming well do, and you're lucky I haven't said anything to Mrs Trent. So just go away, preferably a long, long way away and forever. It was a wicked thing to do."

"I know. It was cruel and evil. I was sorry the minute I'd done it and tried to pick the nuts up again, but I must have missed some. Then I heard about Flame's colic and I was sick at what I'd done. I've had nightmares about it ever since, and I've been trying to screw up my courage to tell you for days. I must have been out of my mind."

"So, now get out of my sight."

"I will. I'm going. I'm leaving the yard for good. I don't deserve to have a horse ever again. But I had to own up first, confess and get it off my chest before I went. I was so jealous of you. You've got everything."

Tears were washing down Amanda's gaunt, pale face. She looked pathetically unhappy and ill, worn out by her burden of guilt. I'd had a good shout to get the anger out of my system, and suddenly I was very sorry for her. I relaxed my over-dramatic pose in front of the door bolt.

"So have you," I said, "got everything I mean. You have good horses, the best possible tuition, and a grandmother who will provide everything you need to compete right to the top. And you'll make it to the top too, because you ride so well. Rich and Vinny told me what a gifted, brilliant rider you are, long before I met you."

"Did they?" she looked surprised. "They never told me."

"They didn't have to," I said, failing to keep the sarcasm out of my voice, "because you never stopped telling *them* and did so much boasting."

"I know, I know. I couldn't help it, then I'd see the looks on their faces and despise myself. But the boasting was a bit like whistling in the dark, to keep up my courage and reassure myself. I was never sure I was any good as a rider, and I was worried that I might mess things up and they'd laugh at me. Gran is always telling everyone how talented I am, but how can I believe her? She's so biassed, and some of the things she says are so stupid. I used to squirm with embarrassment when she was shouting down the instructors and praising me in front of everyone, then I'd feel ashamed because she is my Gran, after all, and I love her. But any idiot could do well on the sort of horses she can afford."

"No they couldn't. Every horse needs riding, and

look how well you've got on with Ebony King. He was hopeless when your Gran bought him."

"He's hopeless now," Amanda said, ruefully and she began to smile through her tears. "I knew he wouldn't make the top grade as a show-jumper the minute I sat on him, but you try telling Gran anything she doesn't want to know!" We were both laughing now, but Amanda's mirth had a despairing, hysterical edge to it.

"Gran was dazzled by the sheer height of him," Amanda went on. "She's an awful snob, and all she could think of was how impressive I'd be, way up there, looking down on everyone. But all she did was to take away what fun I had by putting me out of everything to do with the Pony Club. I told Gran so the other day. I told her that Ebony King would be lucky to make local Opens, yet alone Wembley. Danny and Mrs Shortland backed me up. It's the first time I've ever dared to argue with Gran and she exploded. She disowned me for ever. She sold the horse and says she wants nothing more to do with me ever, because I'm stupid and ungrateful."

Amanda was crying again and I had to suppress my first instinct to be rude about her Gran. Most of Amanda's grief came from the loss of the old battle-axe's friendship, and blood is, after all, thicker than water.

"Look, Amanda," I said carefully, "I think it's a very good thing if you and your Gran don't see each other for a while. She may have meant well, but she's messed your life up in quite a big way. Give her time to cool down and have a good think. She must realise that you are growing up and have your own life to lead, and she can't go on living out her horsey ambitions through you. I'm sure you'll be able to talk it out with her later, when she's got over her anger, then she will understand."

"Perhaps," Amanda sounded doubtful. "But up to now she's done all the talking, I've had no choice but to be only a listener."

"It's time you changed then. Have confidence in yourself. You're a good rider and she can still be proud of you, but on your terms." Amanda mopped at her streaming eyes, and I sensed that she was mentally squaring her shoulders, emerging from the overpowering shadow of her grandmother to reorganise her own life.

"Come to Chawton Show with us tomorrow," I said, on an impulse. "I'll explain to the others. Knowing them they'll be sympathetic. I'll stand by you and you'll have all of us as friends to give you support."

"I very much doubt it. Not after the sugar beet!"

"I've told no one about that, except for Cathy and Charlie, and they won't say a word."

Amanda was amazed and began to get over-emotional again. It took me a long time and several cups of tack room coffee to calm and reassure her but, in the end, she agreed to meet me in the yard the next morning. She left, a friend rather than a dangerous enemy and looking almost human once more.

FOURTEEN

Having sorted things out with Amanda, I felt as if one of the huge weights had been lifted off my shoulders. I was impatient for the phone call from Charlie that might bring me further relief. Cathy had managed to catch him at the Youth Hostel, and told him of our discovery about Burning Red which changed everything. By now, he should have had time for a long talk with the Reverend Threadgold.

The phone rang during our evening meal and I snatched it up, hoping it was Charlie.

"Hello, Rachel love," Uncle Derry's voice boomed down the line. "This is intriguing. Did you know all along that the stallion Burning Red was related to Flame, generations back?"

"I guessed. What have you found out about him?"

"Not all that much, I'm afraid, he's a bit of an enigma. One thing is certain though, he must have been the spitting image of Flame, a lot taller but exactly the same colour. He was quite famous, won masses of races on the flat and earned himself the nick-name of the Red Streak! For some reason, he was retired to stud early, just before he could take the Classics by storm. I couldn't bear to do such a thing if I were training a great horse like that. But there's no record of him ever siring anything, which is very strange. Such a waste, too."

"I think he had to be destroyed before he could be used at stud. What about his form steeplechasing?"

"Don't be daft, girl, everybody knows that line didn't jump. I looked it up, just to make sure, and I was quite right. Jet propelled they were, but none of them had a clue how to leave the ground. The 'Reds' didn't start jumping till they brought in the Flambeaux mares. Like Flame's great grandma, Flambeau Fleur-de-Lis. Now she could jump! Clear a house she could."

"Burning Red was bought by a Lord Swayle," I said. "He paid a king's ransom for him apparently. He wanted to breed steeplechasers, and Burning Red was to be his foundation stallion."

"Then the man was a fool," Uncle Derry snorted derisively. "Lord Swayle was conned, no doubt about it. Doubt if the animal could jump a pole on the ground!"

That was all Uncle Derry had managed to find out, and I'm afraid I left him wondering why I wanted to know! I guessed that no one had deliberately set out to trick Lord Jasper Swayle. I could imagine the overbearing, spoilt young lord taking a fancy to the Red Streak, and bullying its reluctant owner into parting with the horse, offering more and more money until he got his way.

At least I knew now for certain what the stallion had looked like, and why Ben thought he'd seen a ghost when he saw Flame. Burning Red's inability to jump was good enough reason for the stud to fail and Lord Swayle to go bankrupt, but the stud hadn't been in existence long enough for any foals to grow up and prove they were hopeless steeplechasers. The loss of the stallion alone must have been enough to ruin Lord Swayle.

It was quite late in the evening before the phone rang again, and the operator asked if I would accept a reversed charge call.

"It's Ben, Ben is the key." Charlie and I both shouted to each other at once but, by now, Charlie knew far more than I did. He talked for a long time and when, finally, I put the receiver down, I sank wearily into a chair and drew a long breath. Having half a story was worse, almost, than having no story at all, but I knew now that it hadn't been all my imagination.

The old vicar had had a wonderful time reminiscing, but the one thing that stuck in his mind was that there had been something very weird about the stables behind Bridge Cottage. A friend of his, a keen fox-hunting man, had bought Bridge Cottage at Lord Swayle's bankruptcy sale, for the specific purpose of keeping his hunters in the Meadford Vale Hunt country. He had had to sell it almost immediately; his horses refused to go anywhere near the stables.

The Reverend Peter Threadgold laughingly dismissed the idea of the stables being haunted. They had only just been built by Lord Swayle, he said, and you can't have a ghost without a history to have a ghost in. Nevertheless, he admitted, they were never used to house horses, or any other animals, ever again. The cottage changed hands several times and, in the end, the stables were chained and locked shut, and left to rot.

But the brook, he said, was a different matter altogether. For a period of several years the brook had had a very sinister reputation. The Reverend Threadgold could remember the village children telling him all sorts of frightening stories, when first he went to Swallowbridge, about a fearful atmosphere by the water and about nobody daring to go near it, especially on moonlit nights. In fact, the wiliest, most daring of the village poachers had been so terrified by something he claimed he had heard near the brook, that he had had a stroke, and was never able to utter another word or poach another pheasant in his life.

Then, gradually, the wild stories about the brook ceased, and the village tradition that it was an evil place petered out and was forgotten. Thinking back, the vicar said, the trouble had cleared up at about the same time as the stable yard doors were sealed shut, but he was sure that it had been no more than coincidence. There was no connection, other than proximity, that he could recall, between Bridge Cottage stables and the brook.

But there was a very definite connection between the stables and Batty Ben. In his youth, Batty Ben had worked at the Manor House for Lord Swayle. When Lord Swayle started his stud, Batty Ben was promoted to become the stable boy who assisted Basher Simms, the stallion man. Ben had looked after Burning Red.

The vicar described the young Benjamin Puddy as a fine, upstanding young man, a very intelligent lad, who was far from being brain-damaged and who showed absolutely no sign that he might eventually lose his mind. Benjamin Puddy was honest, hard-working and devoted to his younger brother, whom he provided for and brought up single-handed. It was sad, the vicar said, that Ben had had no other family to worry about him and make enquiries, when he disappeared so suddenly.

Everyone in the village believed that Benjamin Puddy had run away to escape punishment. Something had happened up at the stud, but exactly what it was, no one ever discovered. Lord Swayle claimed that it was all Ben's fault: Ben had caused the accident in which the stallion Burning Red had been seriously injured, so was directly responsible for the horse having to be shot. No wonder, everyone agreed, Ben had run away.

Ben's younger brother, Jeremiah George Puddy, vanished at the same time and it was thought that he had gone with Ben, but he hadn't. A month later, his drowned body was found several miles away in the leet of Meadford Mill. What had happened seemed obvious to the people of Swallowbridge: the boy had been devastated, when he discovered that his guardian brother had deserted him, and he had committed suicide by jumping into the mill race. With the sin of self-destruction on his soul, Jeremiah George could not be buried in consecrated ground, so he had been laid to rest outside the churchyard wall, hastily and with never a word of blessing said over him.

I sat by the phone, thinking, for a long time. It was a sad, disturbing story and still, unhappily, incomplete. Yes, there had been a drowning, but at the wrong time and in the wrong place. It could not be Jeremiah George's death scream that haunted me by the brook.

One piece of the puzzle was missing still, and it was, I knew, the most important piece. What had happened when the yard doors were opened and the stallion, Burning Red, was let out to meet his fatal accident? Only one person would know. Benjamin Puddy, Batty Ben, Ben the one-time stable boy in the little yard behind Bridge Cottage, was the only living being on earth who knew the truth.

Many cruel years had aged the fine, upstanding young man into a mindless old wreck. But, buried in his clouded memory was the key that would unlock the mystery and free me from the fear by the water. Now, it was all up to Ben.

FIFTEEN

How could I go through the whole day at Chawton Show and concentrate on the team jumping class, with the unresolved question of Ben on my mind? It would be impossible. I knew that I must find him early in the morning, even if I had only time for a short talk with him. The biggest hurdle would be to make friends with him, to get him to like and trust me, and the sooner I started on that, the better.

I was sure that the Trents would be up early on a show day so, shortly after six o'clock in the morning, I phoned Cathy. I told her briefly about Amanda, and asked her to get someone to sew in Flame's plaits in case I was late. Cathy was bubbling over with the news about Ben that Charlie had passed on to her after he had phoned me, and I don't think she was very interested in Amanda.

"I guessed that you'd want to start work on Ben as soon as possible," she said, "so I've already plaited Flame. Don't worry about him, but if you want Rich and Vinny to be nice to Amanda, you'll have to wave one heck of a magic wand!"

"You wave it," I ordered.

The old folks' bungalows were in the middle of the village, down a little cul-de-sac behind the Post Office and Stores. I didn't know which one Ben lived in, so I knocked on the warden's door. She was a bit grumpy to be disturbed so early in the morning, but when she recognised me from my visit to the day centre, she became more helpful.

"Old Batty is in number eight," she said, "or was. He hasn't half led me a dance this last week, I can tell you. I shouldn't say it, but it's a bit of a relief that he won't be coming back, poor old codger!"

"Won't be coming back, what do you mean?" I asked, startled.

"Took real bad he was. His own fault, traipsing about the countryside night and day in all weathers, moaning about some fire or other and getting himself into a real state! Caught a chill, he did. I couldn't keep him in bed, and then he went down with pneumonia. They carted him off to Chawton Hospital yesterday and the Doc said he wouldn't last the night. Happy release if you ask me, I mean, he's never been all there and he's been dead miserable lately."

My feet dragging with despair, I walked back to Bridge Cottage and phoned the hospital. I was expecting the worst, but Ben was still alive.

"I don't think he'll last much longer though," the ward sister said, "and it will be a happy release for him. His mind has completely gone and he's very distressed about being burnt or something, we can't make any sense of it. Oh yes, you can visit him any time, he's in a side ward."

If one more person talked about 'a happy release', I would scream. Ben's going would leave me without hope of ever knowing the truth. I grabbed my purse and coat, and ran in side-stitching panic all the way to the Rectory.

"Ben's in hospital and he's dying," I panted, as I ran into Talisman's box. Cathy looked up from bandaging the pony's legs. "Oh *no*!"

"I'm going to the hospital to see him now," I said urgently "I don't know how long it will take, but I doubt if I'll make the show."

"You're WHAT?" Rich roared. He and Vinny had come through the coach house door in time to overhear me. "You can't! What about the team jumping? You can't just leave us in the lurch. Go and see him afterwards!"

"That'll be too late!"

"I've never heard *anything* so ridiculous." Vinny was aghast. "What's Batty Ben to you anyway?"

"Very, important, believe me," Cathy answered for me. "Rachel has no choice. She's got to go."

"But the jumping," Vinny wailed. "The *team*!"

"The team will be OK," I told her. "Amanda will ride Flame."

"*Me*?" Amanda appeared in the doorway. "Ride *Flame*?" She gaped.

"Flame will go brilliantly for anyone who rides as well as you do, Amanda," I said, "so don't stand any nonsense from him, and don't let the team down."

"You mean, you'd trust me with Flame after what I

did to him?" Amanda didn't know whether to laugh or cry. I thought it might be the latter and had no time to spare for an emotional scene.

"Look, just get on with it, will you," I shouted." I've got troubles of my own, so stop adding to them and just *do* it!"

"What exactly did she do to Flame?" Rich wanted to know.

"Nothing," Cathy said firmly. She took charge. "Amanda, you'll need clean jods, a white shirt and a black jacket. If you haven't got yours here, beg, borrow or steal, and be quick about it. Vinny, get some travelling gear onto Flame. Rich, start loading the tack into the lorry. MOVE all of you, or we'll be late leaving."

They were all so surprised by Cathy's out of character bossiness, that they obeyed without further question. Amanda hurried after them, the colour slowly returning to her face.

"Rather you than me, and I'll keep my fingers crossed," Cathy said. "The market day bus will be through the village at any minute. Just wave at it and it'll stop. Good luck."

I fled.

The nurse ushered me into the side ward, gave me a busy, empty smile and crackled away in her starched uniform. Ben looked small and lost in the high, iron bed, and infinitely old. His face was sunken and grey, and his breath came in laboured gasps. His hands lay outside the sheet, arranged neatly, one on either side of his body, by the tidy minded nurse, but they shook slightly all the time.

"Ben," I said, as I pulled a chair close to the bed and sat down. "Ben, it's me, Rachel from Bridge Cottage. I've come to talk to you."

His eyes opened, but their stare was unfocussed and vacant, while his slack jaw and wet chin gave him an idiot look. I began to wonder if my visit was just a waste of time. Even when well, Ben made little sense, but now, probably only hours from death, Ben seemed to be beyond my reach.

I began to talk slowly and clearly, telling a story as if to a child. It was a story about a wicked Lord of the Manor and his stud farm, about the Burning Red stallion and the stable boy who looked after him, and then about the stallion's accident and how the stable boy was blamed and ran away. Ben's eye's showed not the faintest flicker of understanding or interest.

"You saw my horse, Red Flame, didn't you, Ben?"

Silence.

"Ben, what happened when you let Burning Red out of the yard?"

No reaction.

"Did he have the accident when you let him out, Ben?"

Nothing.

But then, out of nowhere, I could hear Ben saying, that first night I met him, "Was it Georgie what made you do it, like he made I?" I thought that the name had long since escaped from my memory.

"Ben," I said, "Georgie made you let the horse out, didn't he? Was it Georgie that beat you and made you hurt?"

As he heard the name Georgie, Ben's eyes swung round to mine. To my utter amazement they were alive with feeling.

"Georgie. Poor little Georgie," he said, with an eternity of love in his voice. "Georgie wouldn't hurt I. You must never say that! He were my brother, my little brother. We was orphans. He were all I'd got. He wouldn't never hurt I, and I'd do anything for Georgie."

I was stunned. Of course, Jeremiah George Puddy, George, Georgie. How could I have been so blind, so uncomprehendingly stupid?

"What happened to Georgie, Ben?" I asked gently. His eyes clouded again, but this time with hopeless tears.

"He's gone in the water. He's gone with The Burning, an 'twas all my fault for letting The Burning out."

"But Georgie wanted you to let Burning Red out, remember, Ben? Georgie made you open those big doors and let the red stallion out. What happened then?"

This time, I thought, I'd gone too far. For a long time Ben neither moved nor spoke, but the twitching in his hands became worse as he fought for breath. Then he struggled to pull himself up in the bed, and he looked me full in the face. It was as if a mask had been removed and I was seeing the real Benjamin Puddy for the first time: a man with all his wits about him, for whom the past had at last become clear again.

"He were but a bit of a lad, Georgie was. I did my best, but it were hard. We were poor an' we didn't eat right. He never growed like, but he were pleased on it. His dream was to be a jockey and he had 'the gift', the gift with horses. But ploughboys don't get to ride they valuable blood horses, an' he'd say to me, again an' again, 'let me ride The Burning, Ben. I'll not rest till I have jumped The Burning over yon brook. Then I'll know I can manage they thoroughbred horses an' race over they gurt fences, then the lordship will let me be his jockey?"

Ben's voice faltered, and I hardly dared to breathe in case I broke the spell. I held a glass of water to his lips and he swallowed with difficulty, slopping more than he drank. He sank back onto the pillows and closed his eyes.

"Did he jump The Burning over the brook, Ben?"

"Poor Georgie, I shouldna' let un do it. 'Twer all my fault, but I loved him, see? There were not much in life I could give him, but I could give him his wish."

"No one blames you any more, Ben we understand."

"Had to wait till dark, when stallion man gone home. Waited for moonlight we did, so The Burning could see the brook. But now Georgie have gone in the water, under The Burning. He were still screaming when I fetched them, but they wouldn't shoot The Burning and haul him off Georgie till they knowed the horse's leg were broke and he was finished anyway. But by then it were too late for Georgie. Then they caught I in that room. The Lordship and the big fighting man, they beat I till it were hurting, hurting and dark. When I woke up, I were over the sea with strangers."

The old man stopped speaking, exhausted, his breath rattling in his throat, and my pity for him was like a pain. Everything was clear to me now. There was no point in my staying by Ben's bedside any longer but, in all that bright, bustling, antiseptic hospital, there was no one else who cared enough to keep him company for this last little time. I took his hand and watched his grey face, as I imagined the full horror of that moonlit night, long ago. I thanked a merciful God for clouding his memory for so long, to ease the hurt.

How well I knew Georgie's love for the thoroughbred horses. I too longed to ride them at speed over the jumps, to race and to win. I shared Georgie's burning ambition to be a jockey. Maybe that was why he called out to me so strongly over the great gap in time.

And I had shared, too, his last experiences: his thrilling excitement and his fear as he rode Burning Red out of the stable yard, towards the wide brook with the huge hedge on its far side. Ploughhorse to racehorse was a big step, so no wonder he was nervous, but how was Georgie to know that the ignorant Lord Swayle was founding his stud on a stallion that wouldn't jump?

I could see Burning Red racing into the fence, then balking, skidding and refusing at the last minute. The lad was hurled into the water and, stumbling then falling, the great bulk of the stallion crashed down on top of him. Lord Swayle was too concerned about his costly investment to give a thought for the boy struggling under it in the brook. In the end, his strength gone, Georgie gave one last, terrified scream and choked his way into eternal unrest, beneath water that was only knee deep.

When all hope of saving the stallion was gone, Lord Swayle vented his fury on the stable lad, who had run to hide in the tack room. He and the brutal prize-fighter, Basher Simms, beat Ben with a cudgel, with a hunting whip and with anything else that came to hand. They beat and crashed him round the room until he was unconscious, and the intelligent, fine young man woke from that darkness to face a life of brain-damaged confusion and ridicule.

Lord Swayle had him shipped off to Ireland, secretly and at once. There, Benjamin Puddy became just Batty Ben who worked in a dealer's yard, so that no one in Swallowbridge would ever discover that their Lord of the Manor was vicious enough to kill a man. They found out eventually, when the Indian servant boy died, but it was too late for Ben and Georgie. Justice would never now be done.

And Georgie, Jeremiah George, in his unblessed suicide's grave? How easy it was for Lord Swayle to have the body carted away and tossed in the leet of Meadford Mill, miles from suspicion and undiscovered for a month.

I was still holding Ben's hand, my head bent and my tears falling on our clasped fingers, when Ben moved again. He gripped my palm with startling strength. When I looked up, his smile was happy and his eyes were clear and full of peace.

"Georgie would have liked you," he said. "You and he have the same feel for they beautiful horses. I knows I can leave you to look after Georgie. Georgie won't never rest till he have jumped The Burning over the brook, but you will know what to do."

With a deep sigh of contentment, Ben turned his face on the pillow and closed his eyes. The harsh, rattling breath stopped and Ben was gone. He was right, at long last I knew exactly what to do.

SIXTEEN

Ben must have been connected to some sort of alarm because, even as the breath left him, a bleeper sounded and nurses rushed into the room. I was bundled outside.

"Poor lamb," one nurse said. "What an experience, she should never have been allowed in on her own!"

"Would you like a cup of tea, dear?" asked another, but she hurried away and forgot me when another bleeper sounded.

I made my way, unnoticed, into the lift and down to the lobby. The hot sun slammed against my face as I blinked into the street, and I wandered aimlessly across the market square. My watch told me that it was only midday and I was surprised; I seemed to have passed a lifetime longer than Ben's beside the stark, metal hospital bed. I had so much to do and so little time. The moon would be full tonight, but if I missed this chance, I might have to wait for a month before I could try again, and there was the chance that my courage would fail me in the waiting.

Chawton was packed and market day busy. Penned animals bawled and stank in the heat, traders shouted from their stalls, and farmers rumbled their usual grumbles as they drank their cider, sealed bargains with a handshake and pocketed their cash.

"Don't miss Chawton Horse Show," screamed an orange poster plastered on a wall. A sticker with 'today' scrawled across it covered the details. The showground was only ten minute's walk away, on the outskirts of the town, and I set off down Market Street without thinking what I was doing.

There is a magic smell about a horse show. It is a mixture of crushed grass, sweating horses, dung, leather and hamburger stalls with fried onions. I breathed it in and felt better. I hadn't a programme, so it took me a while to find the ring in which the team jumping was being held.

They were all there, the people who had come to mean so much to me in such a short time. Liz Trent was laughing and waving her arms above her head, while Eve Littleton, Dot Richards and the Bryant sisters were slapping her on the back, yelling and cheering. Inside the roped-off ring, three teams were parading at a brisk canter.

At the front of the procession, Cathy and Amanda, sweating in their black jackets, were having a struggle to hold the enormous, silver cup in the air between them. Talisman was squealing his excitement between bucks and my hot-red horse showed off outrageously. Behind them, Pearly seemed hardly to touch the ground, and the Wizard was wisely keeping out of the way of her plunges. All four ponies were having to peer through the fluttering ribbons of the enormous, multi-tiered, red rosettes clipped to their brow bands.

"We, won!" Cathy called, unnecessarily, when I

met them in the collecting ring, "and your horse was a star!"

"Probably because he was ridden so well." Vinny's voice held unexpected warmth, and I thought that Cathy must have waved a very effective magic wand, after all.

"I mean, Amanda had never ridden Flame before," Vinny went on, "and she had only a very little time to get used to him before we were in the ring. All Flame wanted to do was act up to the crowd, and she did well to sort him out. Honestly, Rachel, I'm sure your horse would rather play Hamlet, given an audience, than jump!"

"Flame was wonderful," Amanda said, "he did all the baton-changing and pairing for me. I was just a passenger. He doesn't fool about when he knows it's serious!"

"I'm finding all this new-found modesty of yours very hard to handle, Amanda Peters. Aren't you going to have just one little boast, so we know it's still you?" Rich said, with a twinkle in his eye. "Passenger, my foot! I saw you drop him one for messing about, then hook him back and put him right at the wall."

"I'm boiled and parched," Vinny complained. "Let's go and get some cokes before we expire. The drinks are on Rich!"

The three of them rode away across the show ground, in a companionable huddle, with Amanda in the middle and the other two heads bent towards her as they talked.

"How did you do it?" I asked Cathy. She slipped from Talisman's saddle and ran up the irons.

"I didn't have to do anything, really, in the end. I

just told them what a rotten time Amanda had had, being overpowered by Granny's ambitions, then we were too busy to give it another thought. Vinny was a bit prickly at first, but she's got a heart of gold underneath and Amanda totally disarmed her. I can't think what you said to her the other night, but Amanda has changed out of all recognition."

"She's a real person at last," I said, "not someone else's shadow."

Slowly, we followed the others in the direction of the refreshment stalls, and I recounted for Cathy everything that had happened at the hospital that morning.

"Poor, poor old man," she said, with tears in her eyes. "So now you know the whole tragic story, what are you going to do about it?"

I told her of my plans and she was shocked.

"But that's madness! It might not work, and what about the risk to Flame? Is it really worth taking such a dreadful gamble? Tell your parents, I'm sure they'll agree to moving right away from the place. Leave the whole gruesome business behind you."

"Flame will take care of himself, he's not stupid, and I owe it to Ben to try. But, succeed or fail, there's one thing we must do, and that's move poor Georgie. He must have a proper burial inside the churchyard, a proper funeral with prayers and things. Charlie's vicar friend will know how to organise it."

"Talking of Charlie, I had a letter from him this morning," Cathy grinned, and pulled a crumpled envelope from her pocket. "Read it, it sounds as if he's having great fun."

Charlie had written from the vicar's granddaughter's

house, to say that he had moved in with the family and would be staying for some time. He and the Reverend Threadgold were writing a booklet on the history of Swallowbridge Village, and were thoroughly enjoying themselves. They intended to sell it in aid of the church roof fund. I told Cathy that I would phone Charlie with the complete story, but would wait to see how things turned out tonight before I did so.

When we caught up with the others, we found that Rich had been bullied into treating hot dogs all round, as well as cokes. Flame's passion for bread rolls was unknown to Amanda, so he had helped himself and had crumbs all over his nose. Amanda was cuddling Flame's neck, and she looked almost dizzy with happiness.

"Saying thank you, Rachel, simply isn't enough!" she said, "and if it wasn't for Rich, I couldn't bear to give Flame back."

"I've had the most stupendous idea," Rich said, through a mouthful of hot dog, "and it solves all my problems too."

"He's going to loan the Wizard to me," Amanda's face was ecstatic. "I can livery him at the Rectory and go to all the shows with you, and do Pony Club Camp and try for the teams, and" Amanda ran out of puff, and everyone was laughing with her.

"Aren't you afraid the Wizard is a bit on the small side for you?" Vinny teased. "After all, he's yards shorter than King Kong!"

"So? I'm yards shorter than Rich," Amanda giggled. "I think the Wizard and I will suit each other fine, and I'll make sure he always has clean tack, which will be a pleasant change for him. This has been the best day of my life."

Although the prospect frightened her, Cathy didn't want me to face what I had to do that night on my own. She offered to come with me, but I said 'no'. I knew I would have to concentrate very hard, to open my mind until I reached Georgie's tormented echo and bent it to my will. Another person there would be only a distraction.

I prepared Flame very carefully, with exercise bandages all round, taped securely into place. It was as if fate had taken a hand when Uncle Derry brought my racing saddle to the Rectory, and I girthed it onto Flame's back, leaving the leathers short and swinging. Flame danced beside me down the dark lane to Bridge Cottage, looking every inch the eager racehorse parading to the start. I knew that he looked, also, exactly like the stallion, Burning Red.

It would be no use trying to make Flame go through the big doors into the yard, which I had left wide open on purpose. I knew he would refuse and become upset. When turned out in the paddock, he avoided approaching them, and a patch of lush, ungrazed grass marked the boundary of just how near he was prepared to go. I led him to the limit of his safety zone, and prayed that the sky would clear soon to reveal the moon.

At last, its pale light crept from behind a cloud and tipped the grass with silver. I told Flame to stand, and I stepped back between the doors so that my back was to the yard and I was facing my horse. I focussed all my thoughts on stopping that violent rush of wind that I knew would come. It must not race its usual course to scream by the brook. I concentrated with every fibre of my being.

The temperature dropped like a stone. I was shaking with cold and conscious of a tremendous force at my back, pressing against me from inside the yard, tingling with excitement. Flame tensed suddenly and flung his head in the air, his ears pricked sharply forward as he stared past me.

"The Burning is out, The Burning is out, now ride him," I said, over and over again in my mind.

A whisper of air passed through and around me, and the pressure against my back was gone. Then Flame took a step or two and checked. His reins, which had hung loose on his neck, tautened into a line from his bit to his withers. The stirrups no longer swung freely against his sides, but were held stiffly down, a little in front of the saddle flaps. But the saddle was empty.

Flame began to walk across the meadow, a riderless horse being ridden. He was trotting circles with his nose dropped obediently to the pressure on his bit, then he was cantering a figure of eight, slowing to a few strides of trot in the middle to strike off again on the correct leg. I was watching a skilled, sympathetic rider getting the feel of my horse: a rider with 'the gift'. And all the time, the excitement in the air mounted, until it was an electric force crackling around me.

Flame was on the far side of the meadow, turning by the roadside fence. He was cantering towards the western boundary, where moonlight struck sparkles on the water under the hedge. His speed had increased to a racing gallop and the impression of excitement was faltering away, first to doubt, and then to waves of fear that washed out to me from the empty saddle of the flying red horse. It was out of my hands now. Everything depended on Flame.

Three strides out from the brook, Flame snatched for his bit, adjusted his stride and powered into the jump. He cleared the wide water and the bristling hedge in one great, soaring leap, and was gone from my sight. There was no point in my running. Whatever I would see on the far side, when I reached the hedge, was beyond my control.

Flame was several yards away in the next field, head down and grazing contentedly. His reins had slippd down his neck and were caught behind his ears, and the stirrup leathers hung limply at his sides once more. The night was warm, still and silent. But something joyous was calling out to me, and I raised my eyes to the moon-misted distance.

Faintly and fading, came the sound of hoof beats and youthful, triumphant laughter.

I was deeply happy as I walked back to Bridge Cottage, down the lane and over Lord Swayle's bridge. I climbed the gate into the next field and called to Flame. He raised his head briefly, then ignored me. He knew that he had earned a leisurely night's grazing after his triumph at Chawton Show and, too, after being obliging enough to turn out at night and jump by moonlight. Nevertheless, I had to know.

Flame clopped resignedly beside me, back over the bridge and up the path behind the cottage. At the same, untroubled pace, he followed me without hesitation, through the yard doors and across the cobbles to his stable. Flame pushed ahead of me into his new home, eager to see if there was anything in the manger.

Epilogue

So, now you know the whole story. I said at the beginning that I would let you make up your own mind about it all. You know that I never actually 'saw' anything only felt and heard things. And no one but myself ever felt or heard anything. Memory is dimmed by time and, looking back, I often wonder if I imagined the whole thing after all. With the exceptions of yourself and my four good friends at the Rectory, I have never told anyone about 'the Red Horse haunting.'

The Reverend Peter Threadgold returned to Swallowbridge with Charlie, in time to conduct a double funeral. Benjamin Puddy and his brother Georgie sleep peacefully now, side by side under the daisy-starred grass of Swallowbridge churchyard, in the quiet corner where the yew trees lean over the wall to shade the rest of the Puddy family headstones.

The local press had, somehow, got hold of parts of Georgie's story, so the little church was packed to overflowing for the funeral service. The national newspapers then decided that it was worth reporting, and the evil doings of Lord Jasper Swayle were discussed and condemned over many a Sunday breakfast table. It was a kind of justice, at last.

As a result of all the publicity, the booklet on the history of Swallowbridge became a minor best seller. Charlie and the Reverend Threadgold autographed copies of it, were interviewed on television and became, I'm afraid to say, just a little big-headed! Even now, Charlie seems to regard the new church roof almost as his personal property, and is forever squinting up at it with a proprietorial smirk on his face.

My year in Swallowbridge flew by all too quickly. It was with great sadness that I said goodbye to the beautiful little stable yard, where Flame and I had been so happy and had so much fun for nearly the whole of that year, and, even though I'm pleased to be back in Lambourn again, I get a little weepy and homesick every time I think of Swallowbridge. But at least my stables are in good hands.

Granny moved into Bridge Cottage. After a tearful reconciliation and a long, heart-searching talk, all was forgiven and forgotten between Amanda and her grandmother. Unfortunately, old habits die hard, and Granny has bought Amanda two intermediate event horses.

"Amanda," Granny said, "is destined for great things in the world of Three Day Eventing!"

Nevertheless, the future star of Badminton and Burghley, still spends much of her time at the Rectory with the Wizard and her Pony Club friends. Granny has learnt enough to be resigned and to play a waiting game, but I'm sure she'll win in the end. I have no doubt that, one day, 'Amanda Peters' will become a household name.

I miss Cathy, Charlie, Vinny and Rich, but we have promissed each other that we will always keep in touch. We take it in turns to write or phone, and it is not too great a distance from Swallowbridge to Lambourn for holiday visits. Charlie is planning to write a book about local hauntings next, and he has asked me to give him a hand with the research. I don't see how I can be of much help to him though, because I don't believe in ghosts. Or do I?